The ship's directional gyroscopes, their work done, fell silent—and instead of their whine there was the thin, high keening of the Mannschenn Drive, whose own rotors were now spinning, precessing, ever tumbling down the dark dimensions, dragging the ship and all aboard her through the warped Continuum. As the temporal precession field built up there was the queasiness of disorientation in Time and in Space and, felt by all the *Faraway Quest*'s people, the uncanniness of *déjà vu*.

But, as far as Commodore Grimes was concerned, there was neither revelation nor precognition, only a sudden loneliness. Later he was to work out to his own satisfaction the reasons for this, for the almost unbearable intensity of the sensation.

He was alone, as he never had been before. In his own proper Time there was the infinitude of Alternate Universes—and, out on the Rim of the expanding Galaxy, the barriers between these Universes were flimsy, insubstantial. In this strange Now into which he, his ship and his people had been thrown there were no alternate Universes—or, if there were, in none of them was there another *Faraway Quest*, another Grimes. He was alone, and his ship was alone.

THE
WAY
BACK

A. Bertram Chandler

DAW BOOKS, INC.

DONALD A. WOLLHEIM, PUBLISHER

1301 Avenue of the Americas
New York, N.Y.   10019

FIRST PRINTING, JANUARY 1978

1 2 3 4 5 6 7 8 9

PRINTED IN U.S.A.

Chapter 1

"Set trajectory, sir?" asked Carnaby briskly.

Commodore Grimes regarded his Navigating Officer with something less than enthusiasm. The young man, thin features alert under the sleek, almost white head of blond hair, long fingers poised over the keyboard of the control room computer, was wearing what Grimes always thought of as his eager-and-willing expression. The Commodore turned slowly away, staring out through the viewports at the opalescent sphere that was, that had to be, Kinsolving's Planet, and beyond that world to the far distant ellipsoid of luminosity, pallidly agleam against the blackness, that was the Galactic Lens. There was no hurry, he thought, no need for an immediate decision. He had his ship again and his own people around him, and little else mattered.

"We have to go *somewhere*," said Sonya sharply.

"Or somewhen," Grimes murmured, more to himself than to her, although he faced her as he spoke. He sighed inwardly as he saw the impatience all too evident in her expression, her wide, full mouth already set in sulky lines. Sonya, he knew all too well, did not like ships, her rank as Commander in the Federation's Survey Service notwithstanding. She regarded them merely as an unfortunately necessary means of transportation from Point A to Point B. There was something of the claustrophobe in her make-up, even though it was well concealed (from everyone but her husband), well controlled. To her the little, artificial planetoids were prisons, to be escaped from as soon as possible. . .

"Mphm," grunted Grimes. Slowly, carefully, he filled and lit his pipe. He realized, as he went through the familiar, soothing motions, that he would have to remind the Catering Officer to make a thorough check of the consumable stores remaining. *Faraway Quest*, with her hydroponic tanks, her yeast, tissue culture and algae vats, was a closed ecological system, capable of sustaining the lives of her crew almost indefinitely—but luxuries could well be very soon in short supply. For example, there were not any tobacco plants among the assorted flora in her "farm." *And was there tobacco growing anywhere in this Universe? And would anybody recognize it if it were found in its natural state?* There was no Botanist carried on the *Quest's* Articles.

"Sir?" It was Carnaby again.

Persistent young bastard! thought Grimes, but without malice. He said slowly, "I suppose we could head back to where The Outsider is, or was, or will be." He chuckled mirthlessly. "After all, we have unfinished business. . ."

"Sir?"

The Commodore looked severely at the young officer. Why was he dithering so? He was the navigator, wasn't he? Up to now he had been an exceptionally good one.

"Where *is* The Outsider, sir?"

Put the Macbeth and Kinsolving suns in line astern, thought Grimes, *and keep them so. Run out fifty light years on the leads*. . . He thought the words but refrained from saying them aloud. Those steering directions had been valid when *Faraway Quest* had lifted from Port Forlorn only a few weeks ago—as Time had been measured by her chronometers, experienced by her people. But the Clock had been put back—not by minutes, hours, days or even centuries, but by millennia. *Faraway Quest* was lost—in Time and Space. Grimes could envisage dimly the sluggish writhings of the matter-and-energy entity that was the Galaxy, the crawling extension of the spiral arms, the births and the deaths of suns and planets. Was there yet Earth, the womb and the cradle of Humanity? Did Man—in this Now—already walk upon the surface of the home world, or were the first mammals still scurrying in terror under the great, taloned feet of the dinosaurs?

"I have the Kinsolving Sun, sir," announced Carnaby.

"If we're correct in the assumption that the world we've just left *is* Kinsolving," Grimes remarked.

"But I can't identify Macbeth," concluded the navigator.

"We have to go somewhere," insisted Sonya.

Major Dalzell, commanding the *Quest's* Marines, made his contribution to the discussion. He was a smallish man, with something of the terrier dog in his appearance and manner. Somehow he had found time to change into an immaculate, sharply creased

7

khaki uniform. He said, "We know, sir, that Kin-solving is habitable. . ."

"It's just that we're rather fussy about whom we share it with," drawled Williams. The big Commander, like Grimes and most of the others, was still in his grimy long-Johns, the standard garment for wear under a space-suit. Even so, in the slightly ludicrous attire, with no badges of rank or service, he looked as much a spaceman as the smartly dressed Major looked a soldier.

"There's no need to *share*, Commander Williams," said Dalzell. "My men are trained land fighters. Too, we have the ship's artillery."

"We have," agreed Hendriks. The burly, bearded, yellow-haired Gunnery Officer was a little too fond of his toys, thought Grimes.

"A world is a world is a world. . ." whispered Sonya thoughtfully.

Grimes said tiredly, but with authority, "Let Druthen and von Donderberg keep their bloody planet. They're welcome to it. After all—we have a ship, and they haven't."

"And a ship," Sonya told him, "is built to go places. Or had you forgotten?"

"But where, Mrs. Grimes?" demanded Carnaby. "But *where*?"

"Mphm." Grimes relit his pipe. He turned to Mayhew, the Psionic Communications Officer. "Can you. . . hear anything, Ken? Anybody?"

The tall, gangling telepath grinned, his knobby features suddenly attractive. "I can pick up the people we left on Kinsolving, even though there's only a handful of 'em. If thoughts could kill, we'd all be dead!"

"And. . . The Outsider?"

"I'm. . . I'm trying, Commodore. But the range,

if the thing is still where we last saw it, is extreme. From outside—not a whisper."

"And from inside?" Grimes waved towards the viewport through which the distant, glimmering Lens could be seen.

"A. . .A murmuration. . .There's life there, sir. Intelligent life. . ."

"Our kind of life?"

"I. . .I cannot tell. The. . .emanations are from too far away. They are indistinct."

"But there's *something* there," stated rather than asked Grimes. "Something or somebody capable of coherent thought. Mphm. Mr. Daniels?"

"Sir?"The Electronic Communications Officer looked up from his transceiver. His dark, slightly pudgy face carried a frustrated expression. "Sir?"

"Any joy, Sparks?"

"Not a squeak, sir. I've tried the N.S.T. set and the Carlotti. Perhaps if I went down and tried again with the main, long range equipment. . ."

"Do that, and let me know if you have any luck."

Meanwhile, the *Quest* was falling out and away from Kinsolving's Planet. She was going nowhere in particular—but on this trajectory she would come to no harm (Grimes hoped). She was consuming power, however, even though only her inertial drive was operating, and to no purpose.

The Commodore came to a decision. "Mr. Carnaby," he ordered, "set trajectory for Earth. Once there we shall have determined where we are, and we should be able to make at least an intelligent guess as to *when*. Bring her round now."

"But, sir. . . Earth. . .How shall we find it? We don't have the charts, the tables, and the ship's data banks weren't stocked with such a voyage in mind.

Even if we hit the right spiral arm we could spend several lifetimes hunting along it. . ."

"We'll find a way," said Grimes, with a confidence that, oddly enough, he was beginning to feel. "We'll find a way. Meanwhile, just line her up roughly for the middle of the Lens!"

He sat back in his acceleration chair, enjoying the sound of the big directional gyroscopes as they were started up—the almost inaudible vibration, the hum, the eventual whine—the pressure that drove his body into the deep padding as centrifugal force became an off-center substitute for gravity. Then, with the Galactic Lens wanly gleaming in the center of the circular viewport overhead that was set in the stem of the ship, the gyroscopes, their work done, fell silent—and instead of their whine there was the thin, high keening of the Mannschenn Drive, whose own rotors were now spinning, precessing, ever tumbling down the dark dimensions, dragging the ship and all aboard her through the warped Continuum. As the temporal precession field built up there was the queasiness of disorientation in Time and in Space and, felt by all the *Quest's* people, the uncanniness of *déjà vu*. But, as far as Grimes was concerned, there was neither revelation nor precognition, only a sudden loneliness. Later he was to work out to his own satisfaction the reasons for this, for the almost unbearable intensity of the sensation. He was alone, as he never had been before. In his own proper Time there was the infinitude of Alternate Universes—and, out on the Rim of the expanding Galaxy, the barriers between these Universes were flimsy, insubstantial. In this strange Now into which he, his ship and his people had been thrown by The Outsider there were no Alternate Universes—or, if there were, in none of them was there another

10

Faraway Quest, another Grimes. He was alone, and his ship was alone.

Suddenly sound and color and perspective snapped back to normal. Ahead shimmered the Galactic Lens, iridescent and fantastically convoluted. It was the start of the voyage.

Grimes said cheerfully, "It is better to travel hopefully than to arrive."

"That's what *you* think," grumbled Sonya.

Chapter 2

Grimes, the acknowledged Rim Worlds authority on Terran maritime history, knew of The Law of Oleron, knew that it dated back to the earliest days of sail, yet had been nonetheless invoked as late as the Twentieth Century. Insofar as Grimes was aware no space captain had passed the buck downwards in this manner—but there has to be a first time for anything. In any case he, Grimes, would not be passing the buck. He had made his decision, to steer for Earth, and he was sticking to it. He hoped, however, that somebody in *Faraway Quest's* crew would be able to come up with an idea, no matter how fantastic, on how to find the Home Planet in the whirlpool of innumerable stars, with never a Carlotti Beacon among them, towards which the old ship was speeding at many times the velocity of light.

"The Law of Oleron?" asked Sonya as she and Grimes, in the Commodore's day cabin, were enjoying a quiet drink before going down to the meeting, which had been convened in the Main Lounge. "What the hell is it? Put me in the picture, John."

"It's an old law, a very old law, and I doubt if you'll find it in any Statute Book today. *Today?* What am I saying? I mean what *was* our today, or what will be our today, before The Outsider decided that it had had us in a big way. You had a ship, one of the early sailing vessels, in some sort of predicament—being driven onto a lee shore, trapped in an ice pack, or whatever. The Master, having done all that he could, but to no avail, would call all hands to the break of the poop and say, 'Well, shipmates, we're up Shit Creek without a paddle. Has any of you bastards any bright ideas on how to get out of it?' "

"I'm sure that he didn't use those words, John."

"Perhaps not. Probably something much worse. . . And then, when and if somebody did come up with a bright idea, it was put to the vote."

"A helluva way to run a ship."

"Mphm. Yes. But it had its points. For example, during the Second World War, Hitler's war, back on Earth, the Swedes, although neutral, carried cargoes for the Anglo-Americans. Their ships sailed in the big, allied convoys across the Atlantic. One such convoy was escorted by an auxiliary cruiser called *Jervis Bay*, a passenger liner armed with six-inch guns and smaller weapons. The convoy was attacked just before dark by a German pocket battleship, much faster than *Jervis Bay* and with vastly superior fire power. The convoy scattered—and *Jervis Bay* steamed towards the enemy, all guns blazing away quite ineffectually. As far as she was concerned the surface raider was out of range—but as far as the surface raider was concerned she, *Jervis Bay*, was well within range. But by the time that the auxiliary cruiser had been sent to the bottom most of the merchantmen had made their escape under cover of darkness."

"Where does this famous Law of Oleron come into the story?"

"One of the merchant ships was a Swede. She ran with the others. And then, when the shooting seemed to be over, her Master decided to return to pick up *Jervis Bay's* survivors. He would be running a big risk and he knew it. The national colors painted on the sides of his ship would not be much protection. There was the probability that the German Captain, if he were still around, would open fire first and ask questions afterwards. The Swedish Master, if he embarked on the errand of mercy, would be hazarding his ship and the lives of all aboard her. So he called a meeting of all hands, explained the situation and put the matter to the vote. *Jervis Bay's* survivors were picked up."

"Interesting." She looked at her watch. "It's time you were explaining the situation to *your* crew."

"They already know as much as I do—or should. But I hope that somebody comes up with a bright idea."

What had been done and what had happened to date was recorded in *Faraway Quest's* log books, on her log tapes and in the journals of her officers. It was, putting it mildly, a confused and complicated story. Not for the first time in his long and eventful career Grimes had been a catalyst; things, unpredictable and disconcerting, had happened about him.

He had been recalled to active duty in the Rim Worlds Navy to head an expedition out to that huge and uncanny artifact known sometimes as The Outsiders' Ship, sometimes simply as *The Out-*

sider. The Quest had carried, in addition to her Service personnel—most of them, like Grimes himself, Naval Reservists—a number of civilian scientists and technicians led by a Dr. Druthen. Druthen and his people had turned out to be agents of the Duchy of Waldegren, a planet-nation with which the Confederacy, although not actually at war, was on far from friendly terms. Waldegren had sent the destroyer *Adler* to support Druthen and to dispute Grimes' claims to The Outsider.

The arrival on the scene of armed Waldegrenese, in addition to Druthen and his hijackers, would have been bad enough—but there were further complications. It seemed that The Outsiders' Ship existed, somehow, as a single entity in a multiplicity of dimensions. It was at a junction of Time Tracks. Another *Faraway Quest*, with another Commodore Grimes in command, had joined the party, as had the armed—heavily armed—yacht *Wanderer*, owned by the ex-Empress Irene, who had once ruled a Galactic Empire in a Universe unknown to either of the Grimeses. And there had been a Captain Sir Dominic Flandry in his *Vindictive*, serving an Empire unknown on the Time Tracks of either of the two Confederate Commodores or the ex-Empress. There had been flag-plantings, claims and counter claims, mutiny, piracy, seizure and, eventually, a naval action involving *Faraway Quest II*, *Vindictive*, *Wanderer* and *Adler*. This had been fought in close proximity to The Outsider—and The Outsider had somehow flung the embattled ships away from it. They had vanished like snuffed candles. And then Grimes I, with the hijackers overpowered and imprisoned, had arrived belatedly on the scene in his *Faraway Quest* and had boarded the huge vessel, if vessel it was, the vast, fantastic hulk, and had been admitted into the enormous construction that looked more like a gigantic fairy-tale castle adrift in nothingness than a ship.

Druthen and his surviving followers had escaped from imprisonment in the *Quest* and had also boarded The Outsider. A fire fight had broken out between the two parties. And then...

And then the alien intelligence inside The Outsider, that perhaps was The Outsider, had thrown them out. Literally. It had cast them away in Time as well as in Space and they had found themselves marooned on what seemed to be Kinsolving's Planet, the so-called "haunted world," somewhen in the distant Past, before the appearance of that long-extinct human or humanoid race who had left, as the only evidence for their ever having been, the famous cave paintings.

Perhaps Druthen and the men and women in his party were the ancestors of those mysterious artists.

"And that," concluded Grimes, "is my story, and I stick to it." There were a few polite chuckles. "Have I left anything out? Anything at all that might have some bearing on our present predicament? Speak up!"

"No, sir," replied a single voice, echoed by a few others.

Grimes, seated at a chair behind a small table on the platform that was a flange at the base of the axial shaft, looked down at his people, at the thirty-odd men and women who composed the *Quest's* crew. They were seated in a wedge-shaped formation, a logical enough disposition in a compartment with a circular deck plan. The burly, slovenly Williams and the slim, elegant Sonya were at the point of the wedge, the others fanned out behind them, in rough order of rank and seniority. The back row of seats was occupied by the ship's messgirls and by

Dalzell's Marines, uniformed in white and khaki.

Like a slice of pie, thought Grimes, *complete with crust*... And then, most irrelevantly,
Sing a song of sixpence,
A rocket full of pie...

But *Faraway Quest* was not, strictly speaking, a rocket, although she was fitted with auxiliary reaction drive, used sometimes in emergencies.

The Commodore noticed that Mayhew, seated three rows back with his wife and assistant, Clarisse, was grinning. *Damn these telepaths*! he thought, but without viciousness. *Get out of my mind, Ken!*

Didn't know you were a poet, Commodore, the Psionic Communications Officer replied, the words forming themselves in Grimes' mind.

Mphm, thought Grimes, and "Mphm," he grunted aloud. He surveyed the faces turned up to look at his. They all seemed to be wearing a brightly expectant expression. So they were expecting him to produce the usual bloody rabbit out of the usual bloody hat...

But you usually do, John. . . Mayhew told him telepathically.

I need help, replied Grimes. *Don't think that I've forgotten that Clarisse got us our ship back*. And, to himself, *That's an idea!*

He said aloud, "I need not remind you how much we owe to Ensign Mayhew and her psionic talents, especially her ability to teleport persons and even, at the finish, such a large construction as this ship. It has just occurred to me that it may be possible for us to reach Earth by being teleported there. What do you say, Clarisse?"

A frown cast its shadow over her rather plump, pretty face. She said slowly, "I'm sorry, sir. But it can't be done."

"Why not?" demanded Grimes. "You dragged

17

the ship from wherever she was, brought her to us on Kinsolving."

"My technique worked then," she admitted. "But only just. . ."

Yes, thought Grimes, her technique had worked—but, on that crucial occasion, only just. Hers was a talent that must have been fairly common in the very remote Past, when Science was undreamed of and what is called Magic still worked. She could trace her descent from a caveman-artist—a painter who, by his vivid depictions of various animals, drew them into the snares, the ambushes, to within range of the thirsty spears of the hunters. But first the picture had to be drawn. Clarisse, telepath as well as teleporteuse and with the aid of her telepathic husband, had succeeded at last in producing a true representation of *Faraway Quest*, drawing upon the intimate knowledge of the specialist officers, the heads of departments and the members of departments. And Grimes, the *Quest's* Master over many years, had, at the finish, supplied from his own mind the essential *feel* of her. *The soul of her*, he thought.

"I would have to paint a picture of Earth," she said. "Or of some part of Earth intimately known to some of you, or to one of you." She added, "I have never been to Earth. . ."

And which of us has? Grimes asked himself. *Sonya was there, on a cruise, not so long ago. And I was born there. But the rest of us. . . Rim Worlders, Franciscans, you name it, anything and everything but Terrans. . .*

"You are a Terran, Commodore," said Clarisse.

"It's many years since I was there," said Grimes. "I've so many memories, of so many worlds. . ."

"I can help you find the right ones," said Mayhew.

18

Mphm. It's worth trying. We can't lose anything. Yet, somehow, Grimes felt no confidence in the scheme, despite his certain knowledge that the girl's talent was a very powerful one, that her technique had worked on several occasions.

He said, "Commander Williams, organize the necessary materials—easel, paint, canvas. And you, Doctor, make up a dose of whatever hallucinatory drug was used before." He turned to Mayhew. "Ken, I'm letting you into my mind. I want a picture, as clear and detailed a picture as possible, of the apron at Port Woomera. . ." He corrected himself. "No. Make it the Central Australian Desert, roughly midway between Ayers Rock and Mount Olga."

"And what was wrong with your first idea?" asked Sonya.

"Plenty. If Clarisse's technique works again we could find ourselves coinciding in Time and Space with a Constellation Class battlewagon. The result would be measured in megatons. The desert's the safest bet, and the Olgas and the Rock are good points of reference. . ."

Sonya still looked doubtful. "Even a tourist coach. . ."

"I've thought of that. I shall visualize the way that things look during the rainy season. As I recall it, there weren't any tourists around then."

He looked down at the upraised faces of his people. He did not need to be a telepath to read their thoughts: *The old bastard's pulling it off again*!

But he could not feel confident.

Clarisse's talent worked across Time as well as Space—there had been the odd business of the Rim Gods, and the equally odd Hall of Fame adventure—but. . .

Chapter 3

It was a good painting.

Clarisse stood before it, sagging with exhaustion, an incongruous figure among her smartly uniformed shipmates, spatters of paint on her naked upper body, smears of pigment on the bedraggled fur kilt that was her only garment. She had dressed the part, that of a cavewoman artist. She had played the part, with a massive dose of hallucinogenic drugs to put her in the proper trance state while she worked. Mayhew, her husband, was beside her, supporting her now that she had finished. She slumped, tired, against him. A dribble of dull red ran from the brush that she still held down his right leg.

But the magic hadn't worked. It had worked before, more than once. It had called the old gods of the Greek pantheon from that distant past when men had believed in them, it had evoked the Mephistopheles of fantasy rather than of religion, it had teleported Grimes and those with him from

Faraway Quest II to his own *Faraway Quest*. It had drawn *Faraway Quest* herself from the unimaginable nothingness into which she had been flung to the surface of Kinsolving's Planet. Now it had failed to transport the *Quest* from the Rim of the Galaxy to Earth.

There was no need for Grimes to speak. Gently Mayhew led his wife away from the easel so that the Commodore could see, in full detail, what had been painted.

Yes, the scene was just as he remembered it. There was the desert, green rather than red, carpeted with the growths that flourished briefly during the wet season. The sky was overcast, with drifting veils of rain, except to the westward, where there was a flaring orange sunset, silhouetted against which were the blue domes—blue only by contrast—of the Olgas. To the east, sullenly smouldering against the grey sky, was the great hulk of Ayers Rock...

But...

But this was how it had looked in Grimes' own time. This was how it *would* look—how many years, how many millennia in the future? The domes of Mount Olga, products of erosion... Mount Olga, a mass of red conglomerate, plum-pudding-stone, shaped by century after century of wind and rain... And even the Rock itself, the granite monolith, could not have resisted the working tools of Time, the great sculptor.

How did the Rock and the Olgas look *now*?

And *when* was *now*?

"Nothin' seems to have happened, Skipper," commented Williams.

"It's not too late to go back to Kinsolving, sir," said Major Dalzell.

Grimes looked at the faces looking up at him. He

21

knew what they were thinking. He had failed to deliver the goods. Mutiny, he realized suddenly, was far from impossible. The Marines would be loyal to their own officer rather than to a mere spaceman, no matter what his rank. Hendriks would probably go along with the Major. And the others? Personal loyalty would influence most of them, but not all. Williams he could count on, and Mayhew, and Clarisse, and Carnaby. . . Yes, and Daniels. But altogether lacking was the support given to any captain by Interstellar Law, by the Regulations of his own navy, or by the provisions of his own Merchant Shipping Act. The Age of the Spaceship—or, at any rate, of the human owned, operated and manned spaceship—lay far in the future. The crew of this particular spaceship might well feel fully entitled to make up their own rules as they went along.

Dalzell seemed to be on the point of saying something further, and those around him were turning towards the Major expectantly. Grimes spoke loudly, more to attract and to hold their attention than because he had anything of importance to say.

He said, "This, of course, was only the first attempt. There will be others. The main trouble is that we do not know, yet, just *when* we are. There *is* an Earth waiting for us." *And how can you be so sure of that, buster?* jeered a little voice in his mind. "There *is* an Earth waiting for us," he repeated firmly. "The only thing to be determined is just what period of its history it has reached." He was warming up. "Perhaps we shall be privileged to see the glory that was Greece." He allowed himself a smile as he quoted from Kipling, "When Homer smote 'is bloomin' lyre. . ."

22

"Homer?" asked Williams. "An' who was he, Skipper?"

Sonya, beside him, collapsed in helpless laughter.

"Did I say anything funny?" asked Grimes coldly.

"No. . . It was something I remembered."

"And what was it?"

"Nothing important. Just absurd. It just came into my mind. When I was last on Earth I spent some time in the north of England. The people there still have all kinds of archaic sports, including pigeon racing. The birds are specially bred for their homing instinct. Oh, anyhow, I heard this story. About a christening. The parson asked the father what name he was giving his son, and the man said, 'Homer.' 'Ah,' said the parson, 'you, like me, are an admirer of the great Greek poet. . .' 'No,' the father replied, 'I keep pigeons.' "

"Ha," commented Grimes. "Ha. Ha."

"I thought that it was quite funny at the time," Sonya told him defensively.

Nobody else does, that's for certain, Grimes thought, looking down at *Faraway Quest's* people. *And what the hell does Carnaby want?*

"Sir," asked the Navigator, "didn't you once tell me about a similar sort of bird that was used in an automatic steering system, for surface ships, on Tharn?"

"Not quite automatic steering," Grimes said. "But the birds were, in effect, used as compasses."

Carnaby turned to Mayhew. "Commander, you're our expert on all forms of E.S.P. Do human beings have a homing instinct?"

"Yes," replied the telepath. "Not all, but some."

Is there an Earthman in the house? thought Grimes. Yes, there was, and he was it.

23

You will have to allow yourself to be placed under hypnosis, said a voice, Mayhew's voice, in his brain.

But who'll mind the shop, Ken?

Sonya, and Billy Williams. . . And Clarisse and myself. We'll manage.

What about Dalzell and his bully boys? And Hendriks?

I'm keeping tabs on them, John. They'll not be able to pull any surprises.

What about your Rhine Institute's famous Code of Ethics?

I'll worry about that when there is a Rhine Institute. . .

Grimes spoke aloud once more. He said, "Mr. Carnaby has given us what may be the solution to our problem. I have seen the records of all of you, so I know that I am the only Earthborn person aboard this ship. At times, in the past, I have prided myself on my sense of direction. I may or may not possess a homing instinct. I hope, most sincerely, that I do. In any case, I have to leave the. . . er. . . technicalities in the capable hands of Commander Mayhew. . ."

Mphm, he thought. *That bloody Major would still like to have things his way, but Hendriks seems to be coming round. . .*

Put it to the vote, John, came Mayhew's soundless voice.

"Nonetheless," Grimes went on, "there are those of us who think that we should return to Kinsolving. I propose, therefore, that a decision be reached by a show of hands. All those who think that we should return, please indicate!"

Only Dalzell and his men raised their hands.

"Those in favour of continuing towards Earth?"

24

The Marines were outvoted. There were no abstentions.

And Grimes wondered what odd sort of rabbit he would be pulling out of the hat this time.

Chapter 4

Grimes was not a good subject for hypnosis. For him the words of the long-dead poet had always held special meaning: *I am the master of my fate, I am the captain of my soul.* And for so many years he had been a captain, literally as well as figuratively. Even as a junior officer in the Federation's Survey Service he had been in command—only of small ships, but in command nonetheless.

Too, this was more, much more, than mere hypnosis. The telepath would be actually entering his mind, working from the inside. Psychic seduction or psychic rape. . . Whatever label was attached to it would make it no more pleasant from the viewpoint of this particular victim.

Luckily Grimes and Mayhew were friends, very old friends. Luckily Grimes trusted, fully, his Psionic Communications Officer. Even so, he didn't like it. Even so, it had to be done.

The Commodore sat in the master chair in the control room, the one from which one man could be in full and complete charge of every operation, every function of the ship. It was only on rare occasions that a captain did exercise such direct, personal control; in normal circumstances there were officers to do this and to do that, to watch this screen and those tell-tale lights. But, Mayhew explained, it was essential that now Grimes, more than ever before, must feel himself to be no more (and no less) than the brain, with *Faraway Quest* as his mechanical body.

Grimes sat in the master chair, with controls, set in the armrests, under his finger tips, with other controls in the waist-high console before him. Behind the console, facing him, stood Mayhew. To one side sat Sonya, with Williams and Carnaby. Mayhew had been insistent that no other members of the *Quest's* crew be present, had been reluctant to admit even the Commodore's wife, his second-in-command, his navigator. "But," Grimes had insisted, "if things go wrong, very wrong, there will be people here capable of taking over at once."

Mayhew held out a small tumbler of clear fluid. He said, "Drink this, John."

"What is it, Ken?" asked Grimes suspiciously. "Something fancy in the hallucinogenic line that the Quack brewed up?"

"No." The telepath grinned. "Just a mild sedative. You're too tense. . ."

"Down the hatch!" toasted Grimes, taking the glass and raising it to his mouth, gulping the contents. He said accusingly, "There should have been an ice cube and a hint of bitters. I like my gin—but not neat and warm. . ."

"It's the effect that matters, not the flavor," remarked Mayhew smugly. "And it's made you drowsy, hasn't it? You've had very little sleep of late, and you're tired. Very tired. Why not admit it? Yes, you are tired. . ." Subtly the telepath's voice was changing. At first it had been pleasantly conversational, now a note of insistent suggestion was becoming more and more evident. Grimes thought, *I shouldn't have had that large, neat gin. . .* Stubbornly he tried to visualize a mug of very hot, very black coffee, then dismissed the image from his mind. He was in this of his own free will, wasn't he? It was just that he hated to make himself subject to another's control.

"You are very tired, very tired. . . Why not relax? Yes, relax. Visualize your body part by part, member by member. . . Let every muscle, every tendon go slack, slack. . ."

S.O.P., thought Grimes smugly. *He'll tell me next to try to raise my arm, and I'll decide that it's just not worth the bother. . . But I wish that I didn't have the sensation of somebody scratching around inside my mind like an old hen. . .*

"Relax, relax. . . Visualize your body, part by part. . . Your right foot. . ."

And Grimes realized that he was visualizing his foot, in every detail—the bones, the sinews, the muscles, the slightly hairy skin, the toes and the toenails, even the texture of the encasing sock and the glossy polish of the black shoe.

He thought defiantly, *There are better feet to visualize*, and allowed his regard to stray to the neatly shod Sonya, to the long, smooth legs gleaming below the hem of her brief uniform skirt. But his own, uninteresting, utilarian rather than handsome foot persisted in his mind's eye.

"You cannot feel your foot any longer, John. You cannot move your foot. Perhaps it is not *your* foot. . . Whose foot could it be? *What* foot could it be?"

And. . . And it was not a human foot any longer. It was a scaly claw, scrabbling on a filthy wooden deck. . .

Grimes was no longer in the control room of *Faraway Quest*; he was in the master compass room of a primitive steamship on Tharn, one of the worlds of Rim Runners' Eastern Circuit. He was looking (as he had looked, long ago) with pity and disgust at the living compass, at the giant homing bird, its wings brutally clipped, imprisoned in its tight harness from which the spindle extended upwards, through deck after deck, to the bridge, to the binnacle in the bowl of which quivered the needle, always indicating the Great Circle course to the port of destination, to the coastal town in which was the nest where the bird had been hatched and reared. The illusion was fantastically detailed; the thin, high keening of the Mannschenn Drive faded to inaudibility, the irregular beat of the inertial drive became the rhythmic thudding of an archaic reciprocating steam engine. . .

And then. . .

And then Grimes was no longer looking at the bird. He was the *bird*. He was dimly aware of the feel of the deck underfoot—unyielding timber instead of sand or grassy soil—and more strongly aware of the constriction of the harness about the upper part of his body. Suddenly there was a greater awareness. It was as though every atom of calcium in his bones had been replaced by those of iron. It was as though, somewhere ahead, there was a huge, fantastically powerful magnet—but not exactly ahead, that was the worst of it. He cried out with the pain of it as supernal forces twisted his body. (He learned later that his cry was the squawk of a bird.)

He thought defiantly, *But I am a man. I am an Earthman.*

29

A scrap of half-forgotten verse drifted into his brain, *Earthmen, shape your orbits home...* Home... And again the scrap of verse, *The green hills of Earth...* The green hills and, vivid against the dark verdure, a flight of white pigeons... Wings beating, beating... And the noise in his ears was no longer the steady stamping of a triple-expansion engine, but the drumming of wings. Wings—and a skein of geese dark and distant against the cloudless blue sky. Wings—and the migrating flock maintaining its course over the black, foam-streaked sea, through the blizzard...

The blizzard and the whirling flakes, glowing white, incandescent against the darkness, the snowflakes that were stars, multitudinous, brightly scintillant in the ultimate night...

The blizzard, the whirling blizzard of stars, and through it, beyond it...

Home.

Again there was the wrenching of his bones, his nervous system, his entire body. That supernaturally powerful magnetic field was not ahead, was not in the direct line of flight. Something, thought Grimes, would have to be done about it. He was, he knew, a bird, a huge bird, a metal bird with machinery in lieu of wings. His hands went out to the console before him. Williams and Carnaby were out of their chairs, tense, ready to take over. There were so many things that could go wrong, that could be done with a dreadful and utterly final wrongness. Nobody knew, for example, just what would happen if an alteration of trajectory were carried out while the dimension-twisting Mannschenn Drive was in operation... (It had been tried from time to time with small, unmanned, remote- or robot-controlled craft, and such vessels had vanished, never to return.)

But Grimes, temporarily a homing bird, was permanently a spaceman.

Under his hand the inertial drive fell silent, the ever-precessing rotors of the Mannschenn Drive sighed to a stop. There was the weightlessness of Free Fall, succeeded by the uncomfortable, twisting pull of centrifugal forces as the directional gyroscopes hummed and then whined, dragging the *Quest* about her short axis on to the new heading.

The persistent tug on Grimes' bones lessened but did not die—but now that it came from the right direction the sensation was more pleasant than otherwise.

He restarted the inertial drive and then the interstellar drive.

He heard Williams' voice coming from a very long way away, "Cor, stiffen the bleedin' crows! I do believe that the old bastard's done it!"

Grimes smiled. He knew that the word "bastard," in Williams' vocabulary, was a term of endearment.

Chapter 5

Inward, homeward bound sped the old *Quest*. Only she and her Master, Grimes, were of actual Terran origin—but humans, no matter where born on any of the Man-colonized worlds of the Galaxy, speak of Earth as Home. Inward, homeward she sped through the warped Continuum, falling down the dark dimensions, deviating now and again from her trajectory to avoid plunging through some sun or planetary system. Once course had been set, however, there was little for the Commodore to do. He would *know*, Mayhew assured him, when the star directly ahead was Sol. "But how do I know," demanded Grimes, "just how far we have to go before planetfall?"

"You don't," said the telepath. "You can't. Oh, you might feel the strength of the pseudo-magnetic field—I have to use language that you non-telepaths understand—increase, but even that's not certain."

Sonya remarked acidly that she had read somewhere that it is better to travel hopefully than to arrive. Grimes, the acknowledged Rim Worlds authority on Terran maritime history, talked about Columbus. *He* had known that those islands which, after weeks of voyaging, had loomed on his western horizon were part of the East Indies. And he had been wrong.

Columbus, said Mayhew, wasn't navigating by homing instinct.

"How do you know he wasn't?" asked Grimes. "After all, if he'd kept on going he'd have finished up back where he started from. . ."

"Like hell he would!" scoffed Sonya. "Neither the Suez Canal nor the Panama Canal was in existence then. Even I know that."

"He could have rounded Cape Horn," her husband told her, "just as Magellan and Drake did, only a few years later, historically speaking. . ."

Nonetheless, thought Grimes, *he had something in common with Columbus. The Admiral of the Ocean Sea, driving his tiny squadron west and ever west into the Unknown, had been threatened with mutiny. And what, now, was the state of crew morale aboard* Faraway Quest?

Mayhew answered the unspoken question. "Not bad, John. Not bad. Most of the boys and girls trust you." He laughed. "But, of course, they don't know you as well as I do."

"Or I," added Sonya.

The Commodore scowled. "You're ganging up on me. Billy Williams should be here, to even the odds."

"He's an extremely conscientious spaceman," said Sonya. "A hull inspection is far more important, in his book, than a few drinks and some social chit-chat with his captain before dinner."

"And so it should be," Grimes told her firmly. "All the same, I wanted him here. He's my sec-

33

ond-in-command, just as you are supposed to be my intelligence officer. . ."

"Not *your* intelligence officer, John. I hold my commission from the Federation's Survey Service, not the the Navy of the Rim Worlds Confederacy."

"And neither the Federation nor the Confederacy is in existence yet—and won't be for a few million years. But I wanted you to flap your physical ears, just as I wanted Ken to flap his psionic ones."

"Nothing to report, sir," replied Sonya smartly. "The troops are well-fed and happy, Commodore, sir. The last batch of jungle juice that the biochemists cooked up has met with the full approval of all hands and the cook. Even Mr. Hendriks seems to be happy. He's doing something esoteric to the fire-control circuits so that he'll be able to play a symphony, using his full orchestra, using only the little finger of his left hand. He hopes."

"I know. And I'm taking damn' good care that it never gets past the drawing board. And the bold Major?"

"He and his pongoes seem to be monopolizing the gym. I'll not be surprised if they start wearing Black Belts as part of their uniforms."

"Mphm. I could wish that some of the others were as enthusiastic keep-fitters. . . And what is *your* story, Ken?"

"I've been. . . snooping," admitted the telepath unhappily. "I realize its necessity, although I don't like doing it. Throughout the ship, insofar as I have been able to discover, morale is surprisingly high. After all, it's not as though Kinsolving were a very attractive planet, and we *are* going somewhere definite. But. . ."

"But what?"

"Hendriks isn't happy."

"My heart fair bleeds for him."

"Let me finish. Hendriks isn't happy. That's why he's shut himself up with his toys, to play by himself in a quiet corner."

"I suppose he's sulking because he wasn't allowed to play at Master Gunner on Kinsolving's Planet."

"That's only one of the reasons. Mainly he's sulking because his fine new friends won't have anything more to do with him."

"You mean Dalzell and his Marines?"

"Yes."

"Interesting. And what about the Major and his bully-boys?"

"I don't know, John."

"You don't know? Don't tell me that your conscience got the better of you."

"No, it's not that. But Dalzell and his people aren't spacemen; they're Marines. Soldiers."

"And so what?"

"Did you ever hear of the Ordonsky Technique?"

"No..."

"I have," said Sonya. "If I'd stayed on the Active List of the Intelligence Branch I would have taken the tests to determine whether or not I was a suitable subject." She added a little smugly, "Probably I would not have been."

"I don't think that you would, Sonya," Mayhew said. "As a general rule it works only on people whose I.Q.'s are nothing to write home about. I'm not at all surprised that it was effective on the Marine sergeant and the other ranks, but on Dalzell... It all goes to show, I suppose, that it doesn't take all that much intelligence to be a soldier. Do what you're told, and volunteer for nothing..."

"At times," remarked the Commodore, "that has been my own philosophy. But this Ordonsky. And his technique. . ."

"A system of mental training that makes the mind impenetrable to the pryings of a telepath. Almost a sort of induced schizophrenia. One part of the mind broadcasts—forgive the use of the term—nonsense rhymes, so powerfully as to mask what the rest of the mind is thinking. The use of the technique was proposed as a means whereby military personnel can be made immune to interrogation of any kind after capture. It involves a long period of training, combined with sessions of deep hypnosis. It does not work at all well, if at all, on people accustomed to thinking independently. I had heard, as a matter of fact, that the top trick cyclists of the Rim Worlds Marine Corps had been playing around with it."

"This is a fine time to tell us. So you just don't know what my brown boys are thinking, is that it?"

"That's it, John. Dalzell's defenses went up as soon as he felt the first light touch of my mental probe. So did those of his men. They're not talking to Hendriks any more, they're just not sharing their childish secrets with him. So. . ."

"So we bug the Marines' mess deck," said Sonya.

"Do we?" asked Grimes. "Do we? Dare we? Would we? Can I order Sparky Daniels to plant bugs all through the bloody ship? Oh, I could—but what would *that* do to morale?"

"I'm no Bug Queen," Sonya told him, "but I think I could knock up a couple or three with materials to hand. *And* plant them, without being spotted."

"All right," said Grimes at last. "You can try—as long as you promise me that you can do it with no risk to yourself. But it wouldn't at all surprise me to find out that some bright Marine has done a course in Anti-Bugging."

He was not surprised.

Chapter 6

Take a personalized finger-ring type transceiver
and plant it in some place where it cannot easily be
seen but from where it can pick up normal, or even
whispered, conversation—and you have a quite effective bug. Have a receiver-cum-recorder tuned to
the frequency of the transceiver, continuously
monitoring—and you're in business. Take a Corporal of Marines who has done a few courses in
electronics and who has been ordered by his superior officer to be alert for bugging—and you're
not in business for long.

Sonya, accompanying Grimes and Williams on
Daily Rounds, had managed to plant two of her
special finger-rings, one of them among the glittering flowers and fruit of the Eblis jewel cactus that
was the pride and joy of the Marines' mess deck—
they regarded the thing as a sort of mascot—and
the other in a ventilation duct in Dalzell's cabin. A
couple of recorders, locked in the Commodore's
filing cabinet, completed the assembly.

Grimes, Williams, Mayhew and Sonya listened rather guiltily to the results of the first (and only) day's monitoring.

Male voice:	Hey, boys! Old Spiky's sprouted a new jewel!
Another voice:	How did you find it, Corp?
First voice:	Easy. The bloody thing's radiatin' like a bastard. The Major thought that there might be somethin' like this left lyin' around. For once he was right.
Another voice:	Ain't no flies on the Major. Can I have a look at it, Corp? Thanks. Oh, here's a thing, an' a very pretty thing, an' who's the owner of this pretty thing?
Another voice:	Need you ask? The bleedin' Duchess, that's who. Mrs. snooty ex-Federation Survey Service Grimes.
Another voice:	Careful. She's not so "ex." She's still a Commander on their Reserve List. . .
First voice:	An' so bleedin' what? I'll spell it out to you. One—we're members of the Marine Corps of the Confederacy. . .
Voices:	We're the worst curse of the Universe We're the toughest ever seen, And we proudly bear the title of A Confederate Marine!
First voice:	Pipe down, you bastards. Let me finish. One—we're members of the Marine Corps of the Confederacy. Two—the Federation ain't liable to

	happen for another trillion years or so.
Another voice:	An' neither's the Confederacy, Corp.
First voice:	But we're here, ain't we? Gimme that ring back, Timms. I'm takin' it to the Major. Thanks. But first. . . Ah. That's fixed *you*.

There was nothing more on that tape but a continuous faint crackling. The other recorder at first played back only the small sounds that a man would make alone in his quarters. There was the clink of glass on glass and the noise of liquid being poured. There was a sigh of satisfaction. There was an almost tuneless humming. Then there was the sharp rapping of knuckles on plastic-covered metal.

Major:	Come in, come in. Oh, it's you, Corporal.
Corporal:	Yessir. I found this, sir. Mixed up in Old Spiky, it was.
Major:	Is it working?
Corporal:	It *was* working, sir.
Major:	Oh. Oh, oh. And I always thought, until now, that the Commodore was an officer *and* a gentleman. This shakes my faith in human nature. First of all, that bloody commissioned tea-cup reader, and now *this*.
Corporal:	Careful, sir.
Major:	You mean. . . ?
Corporal:	Yes, sir.
Major:	Why the hell didn't you say so before?

And that was all, save for minor scrapings and scufflings that told of a search being made. It was not a long one; presumably the Corporal had some

sort of detecting equipment. And then the second transceiver went dead.

Sonya sighed, "Oh, well. It was a good try."

"A try, anyhow," said Grimes.

"An' you'd better not try again," warned Williams. "Come to that, it'll be as well if you don't come with us again on Rounds—not in Marine country, anyhow. Those bastard's be quite capable of rigging a booby trap, just out o' spite. Somethin' that'd look like a perfectly normal shipboard accident." He laughed. "There's an old saying. Listeners never hear good o' themselves! We learned the truth of that!"

"We also learned," said Mayhew, "that our brown boys aren't as smart as they think they are. If they were really bright they wouldn't have let us know that they'd found the bugs." Then he muttered something, in a hurt voice, about "commissioned tea-cup readers."

"But we're no forrarder," said Grimes glumly.

And you can say that again, he told himself. In the old days, the good old days of wooden ships and sail, the Marines had been the most trusted and most trustworthy personnel aboard a vessel, being berthed between the quarterdeck and the seamen's mess decks, a sea-borne police force, ever on guard against mutiny.

But now. . .

Then the Commodore allowed himself a faint smile. After all, a certain Corporal Churchill had been among the *Bounty* mutineers.

"What are you grinning about?" demanded Sonya.

"Nothing," he said. "Nothing at all, Mrs. Bligh."

Chapter 7

Inward, homeward bound sped the old *Quest*, boring through the warped Continuum, dragged down
the dark dimensions by the tumbling, ever-precessing rotors of her interstellar drive. Inward she ran,
in from the Rim, in from the frontier of the ultimate dark—and yet, paradoxically, inward to the
Unknown. Past suns—yellow, and white, and blue,
and ruddy, dwarfs and giants—she scudded, driving
through the stellar maelström like a bullet through
a snowstorm. Planetary systems she passed in her
flight—and on none of them, so far as could be determined, had intelligence yet engendered advanced
technology. There was life, said Mayhew, on most
of those worlds—and intelligent life on some of
them. There was life, intelligent life, but, so far as
he could determine by his monitoring of stray, ran-
dom thoughts, none of those races had yet
progressed beyond the level of the nomadic hunter,
the primitive agriculturalist—and none of them had
yet produced a trained telepath. Daniels, the Elec-

tronic Communications Officer, was less definite than his psionic rival. He was able to say that nobody in the worlds that they passed was using the Carlotti Communications System or its equivalent but told Grimes that the *Quest's* Mannschenn Drive would have to be shut down before any NST—Normal Space-Time—radio signals could be received. Mayhew, however, had been so firm in his opinions that it was obvious that such an investigation would be only a waste of time.

And so we're the first. . . thought Grimes. *The first spaceship. . .* A fragment of archaic poetry came into his mind.

We were the first that ever burst
Into that silent sea. . .

Then he remembered the fate of Coleridge's Ancient Mariner. *There had just better not be any shooting of albatrosses,* he told himself firmly.

Inward sped the *Quest,* and the Commodore realized that her voyage would soon be over. He could feel, in his bones, that Earth was getting close. Not the next sun, nor the next, but the one after that would be Sol. He didn't know how he knew—but he *knew*.

Nonetheless, he wanted to be able to rely upon more than a hunch. He told Carnaby to have all of *Faraway Quest's* surveying instruments in readiness. "Look for nine planets," he said. "Or possibly ten. . ."

"*Ten,* sir? I thought that the Solarian System had only nine planets."

"So it does—in *our* time. But this is not our time. The so-called Asteroid Belt, the zone of planetary debris between the orbits of Mars and Jupiter, was once a sizeable world. Perhaps, *when* we are now, it is still a sizeable world. . ."

"Nine planets, then, sir. Possibly ten. Any other speical features?"

"You've never been to Earth, have you, Mr. Carnaby?"

"No, sir."

"As you should know, the sixth planet—or possibly, the seventh—is one of the wonders of the Universe. Saturn is not the only gas giant, of course, neither is it the only planet with rings—but it is the most spectacular."

"A ringed planet, then. And earth itself? Any special thing to look for?"

"Yes. One satellite. One natural satellite, that is. A big one. More of a sister world than a moon."

"Should be easy enough to identify, sir. But there's just one more point. There aren't any charts of Earth in the ship's memory bank."

"We didn't know that we should be coming this way, did we? But I think that I shall be able to draw some maps of sorts from memory. How much use they'll be depends on how far back we are in the Past. . ."

"Surely the effects of erosion shouldn't be all that great, sir."

Grimes sighed. Carnaby was a good spaceman, an excellent navigator—and a trade-school boy. He was qualified, very well qualified to guide a ship between worlds, but knew nothing of the forces that had shaped, that were still shaping, those worlds. His specialized education had taught him his job and no more. Of what use to a navigator was knowledge of cataclysmic epochs of mountain building, of the effects of climatic change with consequent variation in sea level, of continental drift?

THE WAY BACK

He said, "We might be able to recognize Earth from the maps that I draw. If we don't, it just might not be my fault."

But Earth was, after all, quite recognizable.

Chapter 8

Saturn, however, was the first member of Sol's family approached closely by *Faraway Quest*. The huge planet was not quite as the Commodore remembered it; the rings were even more spectacular than they had been (would be) in his proper time. It was while he and most of his crew were admiring the fantastically splendid sight that Daniels, able at last to listen out on his NST equipment, reported the reception of radio signals that seemed to be emanating from one of the inner worlds.

Reluctantly, Grimes, accompanied by Sonya and Mayhew, left the control room, went down to the compartment in which the main receivers and transmitters were housed. He stood beside the little radio officer who, hunched over his controls, was making fine adjustments, listening intently to the eerie whisperings that drifted from the speaker. They could have been music; there was an odd sort of rhythm to them. They could have been speech, something so prosaic as a weather report or a news bulletin. One thing was certain; they issued from no human throat.

Grimes turned to Sonya. "What do you make of it?"

"What am I supposed to make of it?" she countered.

"I'm asking you. You're the family linguist."

"It's no language that I've ever heard, John."

"Mphm." After all, thought Grimes, he had been expecting rather too much from his wife. He turned to Daniels. "Can you get a bearing, Sparky?"

"I'm trying now, sir. . . 177 relative. . . 180. . . 185. . . Damn it, it keeps changing. . ."

The Commodore laughed. " 'Relative' is the operative word. We're in orbit about Saturn, you know, maintaining a fixed attitude relative to the planet's surface. . ." He pulled his empty pipe from his pocket, played with it. He would have liked to have filled and lit it, but tobacco, now, was severely rationed. He visualized the planetary setup as he had studied it in the *Quest*'s big plotting tank. At this moment the ship was still on the sunward side of Saturn. Inward from her, almost in a straight line, were Mars and Earth. Radio broadcasts—from Earth? In a non-human language? Had there, after all, been pre-human cultures, civilizations? Intelligent dinosaurs, for example? Had it been such a good idea to return to Earth?

But what about Mars? A few artifacts had been found on that world, if artifacts they were. Time-corroded and -eroded they could well have been no more than fragments of meteoric metal roughly shaped over the millennia by natural forces. There had been the so-called Venus of Syrtis Major, a piece of alloy resembling bronze that had the likeness, the very crude likeness, to a woman, that

47

bore far less semblance to the form of a woman than did the famous Colossus of Eblis, the huge, wind-sculptured monolith in the Painted Badlands of that world, to the figure of a man.

"Ken," said Grimes to Mayhew, a little reproachfully, "Sparky's picking up someone. Or something. What have *you* to report?"

The telepath flushed. "I've already told you, sir, that there's life, intelligent life, human life in towards the sun from our present position."

"That. . . noise isn't human," said Sonya.

"No. . ." admitted Mayhew. His face assumed a faraway expression. Grimes did not need to be told what he was doing. He would be mobilizing his department, putting it on full alert. He would be talking—wordlessly, telepathically—to Clarisse, still in the control room, informing her and instructing her. He would be awakening his psionic amplifier, the naked brain of a dog that floated in its tank of nutrient fluids in his quarters. Soon the three brains—the man's brain, the woman's brain and the dog's brain—would be functioning as one powerful receiver, reaching out from the ship, sensitive to the faintest whisper. Psionic transmission and reception was practicable across light years; surely Mayhew and his team would be capable of picking up signals from a source only light minutes distant.

Mayhew said, his voice barely audible, "Yes. There is a. . . whispering. I. . . I was not listening for it, until now. I was—forgive me for borrowing your technicalities, Sparky—tuned in to the psionic broadcast from Earth. That's human enough. Raw emotions: hate, fear, lust. Thirst and hunger. The satisfaction of animal appetites. *You* know. But there *is* something else. Not fainter. Just on a different. . . frequency. I can *feel* it now. It's more. . . civilized? More. . . intellectual. How can

48

I put it it? Yes. . . This way, perhaps. Once, I was present at a chess tournament. All the Rim Worlds masters were competing, and there were masters from other worlds. I shouldn't have. . . snooped, but I did. I couldn't resist the temptation. It was. . . fascinating. To *feel* those cold minds ticking over, playing their games many moves in advance, their Universe no more (and no less) than tiers of checkered boards, inhabited only by stylized pieces. . ."

"Chess," said Grimes, "is a very old game."

"I used chess," Mayhew told him, "only as an analogy."

"Never mind the parlor games," snapped Sonya. "What you're trying to tell us, Ken, is that there's a highly developed civilization in towards the sun from where we are now. Right?"

"Right."

"And it could be on Earth?"

"I. . . I don't think so. The images, the images that I can pick up, the visual images, the sensory images, are. . . vague. The people are humanoid, I think. But not human. Definitely not human. And I get the impression of a world that's mainly desert. A dying world. . ."

"Mars?" murmured Grimes. Then, more definitely, "Mars."

The return to Earth could wait, he thought. On the Home Planet there would be, as yet, no organized science, no scientists. On Mars, if Mayhew were to be believed (and there was no reason why he should not be), there would be no shortage of either. Scientists, even alien scientists, could do more to help *Faraway Quest*'s people than high priests or shamans.

He said, "We set trajectory for Mars. The Martians may not be human, but they'll be more our kind of people than Stone Age savages on Earth."

"You hope. . ." said Sonya sardonically.

"I know," he replied smugly.

"I. . . I'm not so sure. . ." whispered Mayhew.

Chapter 9

Provided that normal care is exercised, the interstellar drive may be employed within the confines of a planetary system. Grimes had no doubts as to the ability of his officers to handle such a not-very-exceptional feat of navigation. So, after the lapse of only one standard day of ship's time, *Faraway Quest* was hanging in orbit above the red planet Mars.

Looking out through the control-room viewports at the ruddy globe he wondered, at first, if there had been some further displacement in Time. Mars looked as it had looked when he had last seen it— how many years ago? There were cities, and irrigation canals with broad strips of greenery on either side of them, a gleaming icecap marking the north polar regions. There were the two little moons, scurrying around their primary.

Said Mayhew, "*They* know we're here. . ."

Demanded Grimes grumpily, "And who the hell are *they*, when they're up and dressed?"

"I. . . I don't know yet. . ."

"Doesn't much matter," contributed Williams, "as long as they tell us that this is Liberty Hall and that we can spit on the mat and call the cat a bastard!"

"Mphm," grunted Grimes around the stem of the empty pipe that he was holding between his teeth. "Mphm." Then, speaking almost to himself only, "What the hell happened—will happen—to those people? The cities, the canals—and damn all there when Man first landed but a very few dubious relics. . ."

"Perhaps *we* happened to them," said Sonya somberly.

"Come off it. We aren't as bad as all that."

"Speak for yourself," she told him, looking pointedly towards Hendriks, who was seated at the console of his battle organ.

Grimes laughed. "I don't think, somehow, that one ship, only a lightly armed auxiliary cruiser at that, could destroy a flourishing civilization with its own high level of technology." He gestured at the telescope screen, where Carnaby had succeeded in displaying a picture of one of the cities. It was as though they were hanging only a few hundred feet above the taller towers. "Look at that. The people who erected those buildings are at least our equals as engineers!"

Tall and graceful stood the buildings, the essential delicacy of their design possible only on a low-gravity planet. Glass and stone and glittering metal filigree, the materials blended in a harmony that, although alien, was undeniably beautiful. . . The sweeping catenaries of gleaming cables strung between the towers, some of which supported bridges, but most of which were ornamental only or filling some unguessable function. . . Green parks with explosions of blue and yellow and scarlet, and all the intermediate shades, that were flowering trees and shrubs. . . The emerald green of the parks, and the diamond spray of the fountains, arcing high and gracefully in shimmering rainbows. . . *Surely*, thought Grimes, *an extravagance on this world of all worlds!* The people, walking slowly along their streets and through their gardens, even from this foreshortened viewpoint undeniably humanoid, but with something about them that was not quite human. . .

"Carlotti antennae," said Daniels suddenly. "Odd that we didn't receive any signals from them while we were running under Mannschenn Drive. . ."

Yes, Carlotti antennae—or, if not Carlotti antennae, something indistinguishable from them. Mounted on the higher towers were the gleaming ovoids of metal, each like a Mobius strip distorted into elliptical shape. But they were motionless, not continually rotating about their long axes.

"Could be a religious symbol. . ." suggested Grimes at last. "After all, we have—or will have—crosses, and stars and crescents, and hammers and sickles, and what else only the Odd Gods of the Galaxy know. . . Why not a Mobius strip?"

Mayhew began to speak, slowly and tonelessly. "They have telepaths. They have a telepath. He. . . He is entering my mind. There is the problem of language, you understand. Of idiom. But his message is clear."

"And what is it?" the Commodore demanded.

"It is. . . It is that we are not wanted. It is that those people cannot be bothered with us. To them we are an unnecessary nuisance, and one that has cropped up at a most inconvenient time."

Grimes' prominent ears réddened. He growled,

"All right, we're a nuisance. But surely we're entitled to tell our story, to ask for assistance."

"What. . . What shall I tell them, sir?"

"The truth, of course. That we're castaways in Time."

"I'll. . . I'll try," said Mayhew doubtfully.

There was silence in the control room while the Commodore and his officers looked at Mayhew and Clarisse. The two telepaths sat quietly in their chairs, the woman's right hand in her husband's left hand. The face of each of them wore a faraway expression. Their eyes were half closed. Clarisse's lips moved almost imperceptibly as she verbalized her thoughts.

Then Mayhew said, "It is no good. They want nothing at all to do with us. They tell me—how shall I put it?—they tell me that we are big enough and ugly enough to look after ourselves."

"Try to persuade them," ordered Grimes, "that it will be to their advantage to allow us to land. There must be some knowledge that they do not possess which they can gain from us—just as we hope to gain knowledge from them. . . ."

There was another long silence.

Mayhew said at last, "They say, 'Go away. Leave us to our own devices.'"

Grimes knew that he had often been referred to in his younger days as a stubborn bastard, and on many occasions latterly as a stubborn old bastard. He had never been offended by the epithet. It was his nature to be stubborn. He was prepared to hang there in the Martian sky, an artificial, uninvited satellite, until such time as these Martians condescended to talk to him. Surely there must be some among their number capable of curiosity, of wondering who these strangers were and where they had come from.

54

"They say," said Mayhew, " 'go away.' "

"Mphm," grunted Grimes.

"They say," said Mayhew after a long interval, " 'go away, or we will make you.' "

"Bluff," commented Grimes. "Tell them, or tell your telepathic boyfriend, that I want to talk to whoever's in charge down there. Whoever's *really* in charge."

"Go away," whispered Clarisse. "Go away. Go away. The message is still *Go away*."

"Tell them. . ." began Grimes—and, "Look!" shouted Williams.

Coming at them on an intersecting trajectory was a spacecraft. ("It isn't showing on the radar, it isn't showing on the radar!" Carnaby was saying to whoever would listen.) It appeared to be large, although, with no means of determining its range, this could have been an illusion. It was an odd-looking construction, with wide, graceful wings. There were no indications of rocket exhaust.

"Like a bird. . ." somebody murmured.

So they've finally condescended to notice us, thought Grimes smugly. Then another thought crossed his mind and he turned to Hendriks. But he was too late to give the order, *Hold your fire!* that trembled on his lips. Invisible but lethal, a laser beam slashed out from the *Quest*, shearing a wing from the Martian ship. She fell away from her trajectory, the severed plane tumbling after her. She spiraled away and down, down, falling like a leaf towards the distant planetary surface.

. . . With my crossbow
I shot the albatross. . .

But this was no time for quoting archaic poetry to oneself. While Mayhew whispered, unnecessarily, "*They* are annoyed. . ." the Commodore barked his orders. "Inertial Drive—maximum thrust!" Acceleration slammed him deep into the padding of his chair. "Mannschenn Drive—start!" He did not know what weaponry the Martians had at their disposal and had no intention of hanging around to find out.

The gyroscopes of the Mannschenn Drive whined querulously as their rate of revolution built up to its maximum. Precession was initiated. Outlines wavered and colors sagged down the spectrum as *Faraway Quest* lurched into the warped continuum engendered by her temporal precession field.

Astern of her, harmless yet spectacular, there was a great flare of actinic light, a near miss. Intentional or accidental? But Hendriks' shooting had been intentional enough.

"I saved the ship," the Gunnery Officer was saying. "I saved the ship."

"That will do, Mr. Hendriks," Grimes told him coldly. "I will see you after we've set trajectory."

"Hendriks saved the ship," Dalzell was saying, in a voice louder than a whisper.

I wish I had an albatross to hang around each of your bloody necks, thought Grimes viciously.

Chapter 10

Hendriks had been stubbornly unrepentant. Hendriks had said, "But, sir, attack is the best means of defense." And Grimes realized that it would be practically impossible for him to inflict any punishment, that in these abnormal circumstances his disciplinary powers were little more than a fiction, still subscribed to by the *Quest's* people—but for how much longer? He was their captain, their leader, only so long as they continued to accept him as such. If it came to a showdown, on how many of his crew could he count? On Sonya, of course, and on Williams, on Mayhew and on Clarisse, on Carnaby. . . Certainly not on Major Dalzell and his Marines. Probably not on Commander Davis and his assistant engineers. Possibly on Sparky Daniels. . .

To maintain any sort of control at all the Commodore had to keep on doing things, had to continue pulling metaphorical rabbits out of that metaphorical top hat. He was like a man who has to keep running to avoid falling over. Well, he certainly had run. He had run in from the rim of the Galaxy to the Solar System, he had run from Saturn to Mars, and from Mars to Earth.

There was no doubt that the world beneath them was the Home Planet. The outlines of the continents, discernible through the breaks in the cloud cover, were as Grimes had sketched them from memory. It was obvious that *Faraway Quest* had been thrown back into the comparatively recent Past, geologically speaking. The polar ice caps seemed to be a little more extensive than they had been (would be) in Grimes' proper time, but there was no excessive glaciation. Probably the sea level was not quite the same, and the mountains might be a little higher—but this was Earth.

Carnaby, acting on the Commodore's instructions, had put the ship into a twenty-four-hour orbit, equatorial, on a meridian that roughly bisected the great, pear-shaped mass of Africa. Then, using the inertial drive, he pushed her downwards and northwards. The Mediterranean Sea, with the Italian boot aiming a kick at the misshapen Sicilian football, was unmistakable, in spite of the drifting cloud formations. It would be early autumn down there, perhaps not the best season in which to make an exploratory landing—but it was in this hemisphere that civilization would, perhaps, be found. The Pyramid Builders? The Glory that was Greece, or the Grandeur that was Rome? Mayhew, unethically reading Grimes' thoughts, allowed himself a faint grin. "No, John," he said softly. "There aren't any pyramids yet, and there's no Acropolis. But there are cities. Of a sort."

"And ships," said Grimes. "There must be ships. I hope that it's not too late in the year to find any of them at sea. . ."

"And where the hell else would you find ships?" demanded Sonya tartly.

"In port, in snug harbors," replied Grimes. "Sitting the winter months out in comfort. In the early days of navigation men always avoided coming to grips with the weather."

She said something unkind about wooden ships and iron men.

Grimes, taking over the controls from his navigator, ignored her. Down he drove *Faraway Quest*, down, down. Carefully, he adjusted his line of descent, aiming for the eastern shore of the Mediterranean, for an imaginary dot on the sea roughly midway between Cyprus and the Palestinian coast. Were Tyre and Sidon in existence yet? Had the Phoenicians emerged as one of the pioneering seafaring nations?

Down he drove the ship, down, down. She was in atmosphere now, falling through the first tenuous wisps of gas, but slowly, slowly. *Faraway Quest* shuddered and complained as the medium through which she was being driven became denser, as upper-atmosphere turbulence buffeted her. But she had been designed to withstand far greater stresses. Through the high cirrus, the filmy mares' tails, she dropped, faster now, but still well under control. White-gleaming cumulus was below her now, a snowy complexity of rounded peaks and shadowy canyons—below her and then, seconds later, all about her, a pearly mist obscuring the viewports.

They cleared suddenly—and there was the sea. Even from this height, white ridges of foam could be seen on the slate-blue surface. And. . . And what was that dark speck?

Grimes checked *Faraway Quest's* descent, held her where she was, then turned the controls over to

Carnaby. Williams already had the big telescope
trained and focused and the picture was showing
on the screen. Grimes looked at it. Yes, it was a
ship all right. Graceless, broad-beamed, with a
single mast, stepped amidships, a low poop from
which jutted a steering sweep. Other sweeps, six to
a side, were flailing at the water. She seemed to be
making heavy weather of it.

"Keep her as she is," said Grimes to Carnaby—
and then, to Williams, "She's all yours, Commander. Look after her till I get back." There was
no need for any further orders. The Commodore
had assumed that a solitary surface ship would be
sighted and had planned accordingly. He, person-
ally, would take one of *Faraway Quest's* pinnaces
down to make an inspection at closer range, accompanied only by Sonya and by Mayhew. The
pinnace was capable of functioning as a submarine—
after all, the *Quest* was a survey ship and carried
the equipment necessary for the exploration of
newly discovered planets. From the pinnace Grimes
would be able to observe without being observed.
And even if he were seen by a handful of ignorant
seamen, what of it? The pinnace would merely be
yet another sea monster to be added to the probably
long list of those already reported.

He left the control room and, followed by Sonya
and Mayhew, made his way down to the boat bay.

Slowly and carefully Grimes eased the little craft
out and away from the parent ship. He looked at
the *Quest* as she hung there, just below the cloud
base. He had hoped that the dull silver of her hull
would blend with the light grey of the cloud—but,
at this range at any rate, she was glaringly obvious.
It was unlikely that any of the mariners would look
up and see her, but it was possible. The Com-

modore called Williams on the pinnace's transceiver and, seconds later, the grumble of *Faraway Quest's* inertial drive deepened to a muffled roar as she rose to hide herself in the vaporous cover.

Grimes brought the pinnace around in a wide arc, intending to land in the sea astern of and to leeward of the laboring ship. It was unlikely that anybody would be looking aft. As he closed her he began to appreciate the situation. The mast was canted at a drunken angle; one or more stays must have parted. From the yard fluttered rags of canvas, untidy pennants in the gale. So her sail had been blown to shreds just before she was dismasted. . . And what was the primitive captain doing, or trying to do, now? Grimes put himself in that seaman's place. Yes, he was hove to, doing his best to keep his bows to the wind and sea. All very well and good, thought the Commodore, when you have reliable main engines, but not so easy when your only motive power consists of sweeps manned by exhausted rowers. . .

But there was the sea, only a few feet below the pinnace, and a very nasty sea it looked, too. Grimes put the little craft into a steep dive, felt his seat belt bite deeply into his body as her forward momentum was checked, as she plunged into the curling crest of a wave. But he had to get down; only a few feet under, the surface conditions would be much calmer. The whine of the pumps was audible above the hammering of the inertial drive as water was sucked into the ballast tanks. Briefly the control cabin viewports were obscured by a smother of white spray that was replaced by a blue-green translucency. The violent rocking motion eased to a gentle swaying.

Grimes extruded the periscope on its long mast. The screen came alive, showing the white-crested seas and, finally, the squattering hulk of the little surface ship. *I'd rather be here than there*, thought Grimes. He put the laboring vessel right ahead, then rapidly closed the range. As he watched, exasperation began to take the place of sympathy. Didn't that shipmaster know the rudiments of seamanship? These might be very early days in the history of sea transport but, even so, several millennia must have elapsed since the first men ventured out from the shore in coracles or dugout canoes. He muttered something about people who would be incapable of navigating a plastic duck across a bathtub.

"And what has he done wrong—or what isn't he doing right?" asked Sonya who, although no telepath, possessed more than her fair share of wifely intuition.

"It's a case of what he isn't doing at all," grumbled Grimes.

"All right. You're the expert. What should he be doing?"

"He's in trouble," Grimes told her.

"A blinding glimpse of the obvious."

"Let me finish. He's in trouble. Unless he can keep that unhandy little bitch's head to the sea he'll be swamped. . ."

"I'm no seaman, my dear, but even I can see that that is what he's doing."

"Yes, yes. But there's a way of doing it that does not involve his oarsmen pulling their hearts out. I thought that the technique was as old as ships, but I must be wrong. Oh, well, I suppose that somebody had to invent it."

"And what is this famous technique?"

"The sea anchor, of course."

"Isn't the sea too deep here to use an anchor?"

Grimes sighed. "A sea anchor is not the sort of

anchor you were thinking of. It's not a hunk of iron or, as it probably is in these times, stone. Ideally it's a canvas drogue, not unlike the windsock you still see used on some primitive air-landing strips. It's paid out from the bows of a ship on the end of a long line. It is, or should be, completely submerged and not affected by the wind. The ship, of course, is so affected and is blown to leeward of the sea anchor, which has sufficient grip on the water to keep her head up to wind and sea. If you haven't a proper drogue, of course, almost anything will do, as long as it's only just buoyant and has sufficient surface to act as a drag." He glared at the periscope screen. "And there's that nong, sweating his guts out on his steering oar while his crew, at the sweeps, must be on the point of dropping dead with exhaustion. Damn it all, I hate to see a ship, any ship, in trouble! If only I could tell the stupid bastard what to do. . ."

"You can, John," said Mayhew quietly.

Grimes laughed. "All right, all right, so that skipper's not the only stupid bastard around here. I forgot that you can transmit as well as receive. Do you think you can get a message to him?"

"I'm. . . I'm trying now. I'm. . . inside his mind. I don't like it much. He's terrified, of course. And it's not only a healthy fear of the elements, but also a superstitious dread. . . He didn't make the proper sacrifices before pushing out on this voyage, and he knows it. The wine that he poured out on to the altar was very cheap and inferior stuff, almost vinegar. . . And the goat that had its throat cut was diseased and no good for anything else. . ."

"Mphm. So if you're going to do anything, do it properly or not at all. But can you get through to him, Ken?"

"I'm. . . I'm trying. He *feels* something. He's rationalizing, if you can call it that. He thinks, if you can call it thinking, that the Sea God is condescending to answer his grovelling prayers. But the superstition. . . It's sickening!"

"Never mind that. He's typical of his day and age. *Be* a Sea God! Prod him up the arse with your trident and make him *do* something!"

Mayhew managed a sickly smile. He said, "I don't like doing it, but it's the only way. . ." He whispered, vocalizing the thoughts that he was striving to transmit, *"Hear, and ye shall be saved. . . Heed, and ye shall be saved. . ."*

"Good," said Grimes. "Keep it up. As soon as you're through to him, *tell* him. You heard me explaining the sea-anchor technique. He won't have a drogue, of course, but anything at all will do. Anything."

There was a long silence, broken at last by the telepath. "It's hard, John, trying to explain modern seamanship to that primitive savage."

"*Modern* seamanship?" scoffed Grimes. "This is going back to the first, the very first beginnings of seamanship!"

"Perhaps the idea of a sacrifice. . ." whispered Mayhew.

"General Average!" laughed the Commodore. "A pity we haven't got a Lloyd's underwriter along to sort it out!" Then, "You *are* getting through, Ken. One of the two men on the steering oar has just gone below. . . Yes. And a sweep on either side has been shipped. . ."

He watched the periscope screen with gleeful anticipation. So the primitive shipmaster was experiencing a long overdue rush of brains to the head—and he, Grimes, Honorary Admiral of one of the surface navies of Tharn, holder of an Aquarian Master Mariner's Certificate of Competency, was responsible. Sonya glared at him as he began to sing, softly and tunelessly, an archaic Terran sea chantey:

"Blow the man down, bullies, blow the man down—

Way, hey, blow the man down!

Blow him away right to Liverpool town—

Oh, give us the time to blow the man down!"

Yes, here they came on deck, a half dozen of them, dragging something. *Take it for'ard, you unseamanlike cows*, muttered Grimes. *Not aft. . .* Then he decided that the skipper probably knew what he was doing; it could be that his clumsy vessel would ride better, would ship less water if brought up to the sea anchor with the weather astern. But what was happening in the poop? Mutiny? There seemed to be some sort of scrimmage in progress.

Ah, at last. The seamen, acting as one, were lifting what looked like a bundle of rags. *"Not big enough. . ."* muttered Grimes. *"Not nearly big enough. . ."* They lifted the bundle of rags and dropped it over the stern. *"And where the hell's your sea-anchor line?"* demanded Grimes furiously.

Then, just before a hissing rain squall blotted out all vision, the Commodore and his companions saw that the thing jettisoned was a man.

Chapter 11

There was only one thing to do, and Grimes did it. But he could not be too hasty; for him to surface right alongside the laboring ship would be out of the question. She was making slow headway against the sea, however, gradually pulling away from that small, dark figure struggling in the water. The periscope was useless in the heavy, driving rain, so the pinnace's fantastically sensitive radar was brought into operation.

On the screen were two targets, one large and one small, and the smaller target was showing only intermittently in the clutter. The range between the two blips was opening. The Commodore adjusted his speed to maintain his distance off from the larger target, steered so as to come directly beneath the smaller one. It was tricky work, but somehow he managed it. Suddenly there was a distinct shock, a continued vibration. Grimes guessed what it was. A drowning man will clutch at a straw—and a periscope standard is considerably more substantial.

Grimes started to blow his tanks, but as soon as the pinnace rose into the layer of turbulence just below the sea surface the motion was dangerously violent. He tried to correct it with the pinnace's control surfaces, but it was impossible to do so. Hastily he turned to the inertial drive controls, switched from *Ahead* to *Lift*. The unrhythmic hammering of the engine was deafening in the confined space of the little vessel's cabin and she went up like a rocket, lurching far over as a sea caught her, but recovering. Was the man still there? The lens of the periscope could be swivelled so that the upper hull could be inspected. This was done—and the screen showed a huddled mass of dark rags wrapped around the base of the standard.

"We have to bring him in," said Grimes.

"By 'we,'" said Sonya, "you imply 'you.'" She unstrapped herself from her seat, and Mayhew followed suit.

"Be careful," warned Grimes.

"Good and careful," she said.

The upper hatch slid open and fresh air—cool, humid, salty—gusted in, and with it a spatter of chilly rain. But after the weeks of canned atmosphere, it was like sparkling wine after flat water. Grimes inhaled deeply and gratefully, watched Sonya clamber up the short ladder and vanish, followed by Mayhew. He heard her voice, faint but clear over the whining of the wind, the drumming of the rain, "Don't be afraid. Nobody's going to hurt you. . ." Surely that pitiful heap of human jetsam would understand the tone if not the words themselves.

Then, from Mayhew, "He's terrified. . ."

"And so would you be. *Help* me, Ken. Get into

his mind or whatever it is you do, and tranquilize him. . ."

"I'm. . . I'm trying, Sonya. . ."

"Then try a little harder. His hands are *frozen* onto the periscope. . ." She continued in a crooning voice, "You're safe now. . . Just relax. . . We've got you. . ."

Another voice replied—high-pitched, gabbling. Grimes thought that he distinguished the word *elohim.*

"Yes. . . yes. . . hold on to me. . . *Give me a hand, Ken, or we'll both be overboard!* Yes. . . yes. . . hold on now. . . Carefully. . . Carefully. . . This way. . ."

First one of Sonya's shapely legs appeared through the circular hatch, then the other. Her feet sought and found the ladder rungs. Her buttocks in her rain-soaked skirt came into view, descended slowly. Between her upper body and the ladder, moving feebly, were a pair of bare feet under skinny calves. She was holding the man so that he could not fall, and Mayhew, above her, had a tight grip on the castaway's wrists and was lowering him as required.

They got him down at last. He collapsed onto the deck, huddling there in the pool of sea water that ran from his ragged clothing. Grimes turned in his chair to look at him. He was obviously a Semite; in this part of the world that was to be expected. He was paralyzed with terror—and that was not surprising. He stared up at his rescuers while his hands clawed at his black, straggling beard. He was trying to say something, but words would not, could not come.

Mayhew said, "I'm getting some sense out of his mind, John, but not much. He's too frightened. He thinks we're angels or something. . ."

"Mphm." Grimes turned back to his controls, shutting the hatch then cutting the lift. The pinnace fell to the sea, submerged rapidly to periscope depth as the pumps sucked water into the ballast tanks. It was not a moment too soon. The rain squall was almost over; in another two or three seconds the little spacecraft would have been clearly visible from the surface ship.

Yes, she was still there, clearly visible through the thinning veils of rain. She was still there, and riding much more easily. This must have been the clearing squall. The wind was dropping and the sea was much less rough and, very soon in this land-enclosed expanse of water the swell would be diminishing. The shipmaster would not be needing a sea anchor now.

"I've got. . . something. . ." said Mayhew. There was something odd about his voice.

"Out with it, Ken," ordered Grimes.

"He. . . he was a passenger aboard that ship. Some kind of preacher. He was bound for. . . Ninevah. His name. . ."

"I don't think you need to tell me," said the Commodore. And he thought, *But we have a temporal reference point. Once we get back on board the* Quest, *with her data banks, we shall be able to pinpoint ourselves in Time.*

Chapter 12

"Well," demanded Grimes irritably, "what have you found out? We haven't much time left, you know. Sonya insists that our friend be put ashore on a deserted beach not one second later than three days after his rescue. . ."

"We must keep to the script," stated Sonya firmly.

"Script? What script? Damn it all, I hoped that by rescuing Jonah we should be able to find out just *when* we are—and what do we find? What does our data bank, our fabulous electronic encyclopedia have to tell us? Just that the Book of Jonah is only a legend, a piece of allegorical fiction, and that the Great Fish symbolizes Dagon or some other ichtyological deity. What does it matter if we keep him aboard the *Quest* three days, three weeks, or three months? Or three years. . ."

"We mustn't tamper with history," she said.

"History is always being tampered with," he grumbled.

"Yes. But not at the time when it's actually happening."

"There has to be a first time for everything," he said. But he realized that they were all against him. None of the *Quest's* crew was religious—but they all had their superstitions. Holy Writ is Holy Writ. And here, under heavy sedation in the ship's sick bay, was living proof that there is more to the Bible than mere mythology.

"Better stick to the script," said Williams.

"It would be the wisest course," agreed Carnaby.

Grimes looked around at the faces of his other senior officers, saw that all of them were in favor of returning the castaway to land. He couldn't help grinning. So the unfortunate man was a double Jonah, as it were, first thrown overboard from the surface vessel, now to be ejected from the spaceship. But it was a pity. Further probing by Mayhew and Clarisse could well have turned up information of value.

"So we put him down," said the Commodore heavily, at last. Then, to Mayhew, "But you must have found *something* out, Ken. . ."

"Given time," murmured the telepath, "we can promise to crack any nut you throw onto our plate. But we haven't had the time." He paused. "How shall I put it, sir? Like this, perhaps. Just imagine that *you* are trying to question somebody with whom you share a common language, but that this somebody is so terrified that he screams wordlessly, without so much as a second's break. . . That's the way it is. Oh, we can read thoughts, to use the common jargon, but it helps a lot when those thoughts are reasonably coherent. His are not."

"So he's *still* terrified?"

"Too right he is. Try to look at it from *his* view-

71

point. He's in the belly of a great fish. He has every right to be terrified."

"Like hell he has. He's being pampered worse than any VIP passenger aboard a luxury liner. Specially cooked meals, served by our most attractive stewardesses. . ."

"Whom he regards as succubi just waiting for the chance to dig their painted claws into him to drag him down to Hell. . ."

"But can't you and Clarisse get into his mind, to calm him down?"

"Don't you think that we haven't tried, that we still aren't trying? Given time, we should succeed. But three days just aren't long enough."

"And the three days are almost up," said Sonya, looking at her watch.

Grimes sighed, got up from his seat, led the way from his quarters to the control room. He looked at the periscope screen, but *Faraway Quest* was above the clouds; nothing was visible but a restless sea of gleaming white vapor. But Carnaby had constructed a chart and proudly showed it to the Commodore. "We're here," he said, stabbing with a pencil point at the dot with the small circle around it. "*Here*" appeared to be over the sea. "And there," he added, "is the city. . ."

Grimes took the pencil. "And we land," he said, "here. As far as we could see before the cloud covered things it's a nice little well-sheltered bay. And it should be no more than three days' not very strenuous walk from the coast to the city. I suppose that it *is* Ninevah?"

Nobody answered him.

"Mphm." He played with the dividers, measuring off the distance. "I still think that it would save trouble all round if I took the pinnace down after dark and landed our passenger right at his destination."

Sonya quoted solemnly, "And the Lord spake unto the fish, and it vomited out Jonah upon the dry land. And the word of the Lord came unto Jonah the second time, saying, Arise, go into Ninevah, that great city, and preach unto it the preaching that I bid thee. So Jonah arose, and went unto Ninevah, according to the word of the Lord. Now Ninevah was an exceeding great city of three days' journey. . ."

"Is the amphibian ready, Commander Williams?" asked Grimes.

"All ready, Skipper," replied Williams.

"Then let's get it over with," said the Commodore.

He handled the small craft himself, bringing her down from the mother ship in a steep dive, levelling off just before he hit the water, landing on the sea about half a kilometer from the shore. He had decided against landing on the beach itself; perhaps to have done so would have constituted a deviation from the script. The little bay was not as sheltered as it had looked from the air; there was a moderate westerly swell running and the pinnace wallowed sickeningly. Grimes was not at all surprised to hear somebody in the passenger cabin abaft him being violently ill. He felt sorry for the native, assuming (correctly) that it was he; the combination of seasickness with overwhelming terror must be almost unbearable. Then he ignored the miserable sounds and the unmistakable reek of vomit, concentrated on running in at right angles to the line of breakers. The aerial survey had shown that there were no submerged reefs to worry about—but it would do the pinnace and her occupants no good at all if she were allowed to broach to, if she were rolled over and over and dumped violently onto hard sand. He applied lift so that the craft became barely airborne; in the unlikely event that there were any observers ashore this would not be obvious.

He skimmed over the surf, steering for a tall, solitary palm tree. He roared over rather than through the shallows. Then, gently, he cut the inertial drive, dropped down to the dry sand with hardly a jar. He turned in his seat, saw that Sonya and Mayhew were standing and were supporting the native between them. The poor devil was in a sorry state, looking at least half dead with fear and nausea. But his troubles were almost over. (Or were they just starting?)

"Take him out, John?" asked Sonya.

"Yes, as long as you're sure that it's according to the Book."

"It has to be," she said coldly.

The 'midships door opened and the little ramp extended itself. Sonya and Mayhew guided the man—he looked like little more than a bundle of filthy rags—towards the opening. He seemed in no condition for a forty-kilometer walk—but he, too, would have to follow the script.

With blessed solidity under his bare feet, with familiar sights around him, he recovered fast. But he fell prone, trying to embrace the earth. At last he sat up, looking down at his hands, through which he was dribbling a stream of golden sand. There was an incredulous smile on his dark, bearded face—a smile that swiftly faded as his regard shifted upwards, as he saw the beached amphibian still there. Hastily he looked away, staring inshore, drawing renewed strength from the prosaic (to him) spectacle of rolling dunes, clumped palm trees and a serrated ridge of blue mountains on the horizon. He got shakily to his feet and started to walk, with surprising vigor, heading inland, away from the accursed sea and its denizens.

"Another satisfied customer," muttered Grimes.

Sonya and Mayhew got back into the pinnace and as soon as the craft was sealed the Commodore lifted her and set course for the waiting *Faraway Quest*.

Chapter 13

Back aboard the *Quest* Grimes went straight from the boat bay to his quarters, accompanied by Sonya and Mayhew. He sent for Williams and Clarisse. She, of course, did not need to be told all that had happened; she had been in telepathic communication with her husband throughout. And it did not take long to put Williams into the picture.

Then, "I intend to land tomorrow morning, at dawn," announced Grimes.

"Will it be wise?" queried Sonya. "As I've said before, and as I keep on saying, we must not tamper with history."

"Have we done so?" countered her husband. "Shall we do so? This last episode has established, I think, that we are already a part of history."

"Never mind history, Skipper," put in Williams. "You look after yourself, and let history look after itself. I'm tellin' you this; unless the boys an' girls get some sort o' break, you're goin' to have a mutiny on your hands."

THE WAY BACK

"As bad as that, Billy?"

"As bad as that. For days now we've been hangin' over one little spot of empty ocean, with nothin' to look at but sea an' clouds. It's even worse than bein' in orbit. It's a case of so near an' yet so far."

"Ken?"

"I should have told you before, John, but I thought you knew. In any case, I've been keeping my prying to a minimum. And you don't have to be a telepath to be aware of the unhappy atmosphere that's permeating the ship. You don't have to be a mind reader to overhear remarks such as, 'He and his pets get down to the surface any time they want to. Why shouldn't we?'"

Grimes grinned humorlessly. "I know, I know. That's why I've decided to make a landing."

"I still say that it's risky," stated Sonya flatly.

"How so?"

"It's obvious. Or should be. *There. . .*" she made a down-sweeping gesture. . . "we have a world whose civilizations, such as they are, are very little advanced beyond the Stone Age. Here we have a ship packed almost to bursting with the technology of *our* time. What sort of impact shall we make?"

"A very light one," said Grimes, "if I set the old bitch down with my usual consummate skill."

She waited until the others had stopped laughing then said coldly, "You know very well what I meant."

"Yes. I know. And I still say, 'a very light one.' Only the very crudest technology would mean anything to those people down there. Anything beyond it will be, so far as they're concerned, magic. . ."

"And isn't that just as bad, if not worse?"

"No. Remember that Terran mythology is full of legends of gods who visited Earth from beyond

77

the stars. Quite possibly some—or most—of those legends are based on fact. Quite possibly *we* are part of the mythology. Quite possibly? No. We *are* part of the mythology."

"Jonah. . ." said Mayhew.

"Yes."

"But how do you know," argued Sonya stubbornly, "that our Jonah was *the* Jonah? After all, it must be a very common name in this here and now. Perhaps the *real* Jonah was rescued from a watery grave a couple of centuries ago. Or perhaps it won't happen for another hundred years."

"Please don't stretch the long arm of coincidence to breaking point," the Commodore admonished her.

"But there is such a thing as coincidence. And I still think that by too-intimate contact with the people of this period we're liable to shunt the world onto a different Time Track."

"And so, to coin a phrase, what?" he demanded.

"Then quite possibly we shall never be born. Not only shall we find it impossible to return to our own Time but we must just. . . vanish. We shall never have been."

Grimes laughed. "And you can say that, quite seriously, after all the peculiar strife, timetrackwise, that we've been in already. . . Really. What about my carbon copy whom we met, not so long ago? Even though *his* ship wasn't a carbon copy of *my* ship. . ."

"And *his* wife far from being a carbon copy of yours. So you'd prefer Maggie Lazenby to me, is that it?"

"I never said anything of the kind. And what about that poor old Commander Grimes, passed over for promotion but still in the Survey Service, commanding that utterly unimportant base. . ."

"I seem to remember that Maggie was mixed up in that affair, too."

"And so were you." Grimes was playing with his battered pipe, wishing desperately that he had the wherewithal to fill it. (Had tobacco grown around the Mediterranean Basin in ancient times, as well as in North America? It would be worth finding out.) "Get this straight, Sonya. There's no possibility of our cancelling ourselves out. From every second of Time an infinitude of world lines stretches into the Future. Some, perhaps, are more 'real' than others. Or more probable. All will be real enough to the people living on them. And we were—or will be—born on at least one of those tracks. At least one? Now I'm talking nonsense. In any case, I'm pretty sure that we shall not influence the course of history. After all, you can't have steam engines until it's steam-engine time."

"And what fancy theory is that?"

"It's more than a theory. The steam engine is a *very* ancient invention. But it was hundreds of years before anybody thought of putting it to work. When Hero made his primitive steam turbine there was no demand for mechanical power. And there'll be no demand for our sophisticated machinery in this Time.

"We land tomorrow."

"That will be the wisest course of action, John," said Mayhew slowly. "So far, all hands are still with you, but there's considerable discontent. All hands? All hands, that is, with the exception of those bloody Pongoes. What they are thinking, I don't know. But they are a minority and quite incapable of taking over the ship."

"You say, 'so far.' "

"Yes. So far. As long as you let your people get away from this tin coffin for a while they'll remain loyal. If you don't, if you keep them cooped up, anything might happen."

"I still don't like the idea of landing," said Sonya stubbornly. "I think that it's asking for trouble."

"Whatever we do is asking for trouble," Grimes told her. "We could return to Mars—and get ourselves blown out of the sky. We could scour the Universe and die of old age before we found another habitable planet. Earth, after all, is Home—and we have come Home. Let's make the best of it."

"You're the boss," she said resignedly.

Chapter 14

The Isles of Greece. . .

That phrase, that scrap of half-remembered verse, possessed a magic insofar as Grimes was concerned. And there were the memories, too, of that odd planet called by its people Sparta, that Lost Colony with its culture modelled on that of the long-dead City State. He would have liked to have seen what the real Sparta was like. . . He could have made his landing in Egypt or in Palestine, in Italy or in Spain, in Carthage—but he decided upon Greece. He was unable to recollect his Terran geography, even with the mind-probing assistance of his telepaths, and the ship's data bank was no help at all, but it didn't matter. The outlines of the Archipelago were unmistakable enough, even if he could not say just where Sparta or Athens stood, or would stand. He relied upon his instruments to select what appeared to be a good landing site—flat, between sea and mountains, on the bank of a small river. The descent at sunrise was standard survey practice; the almost level rays of light would show up every irregularity and then, once the landing had been made, there would be a full day to get settled in—or during which to decide to get the hell out.

Slowly, carefully, Grimes brought *Faraway Quest* down through the still, clear morning air. As the ship lost altitude he could see streamers of blue smoke rising almost vertically a little to the north of where he had decided to land. Cooking fires? A village? Carnaby stepped up the magnification of the periscope screen and the huddle of huts along a bend in the river could be seen clearly.

And what of the villagers? Surely they must have heard by this time the uncanny thunder beating down from a clear sky; surely they must have seen the great, gleaming shape dropping down from the heavens. *And had this event, or similar events, given the ancient Greek dramatists their favourite, labor-saving gimmick, the* deus ex machina? Grimes smiled at the thought. It was odd, though, that this convention existed only in Greek drama.

Yes, there were people. And they had come out into the open, were not cowering under cover. They were standing there, outside their huts, staring upwards. Grimes was tempted to use his reaction drive to give them a show for their money, but restrained himself. A sudden display of dazzling, screaming fire could well engender panic. It was amazing that there was no panic already.

Not allowing his attention to stray from his instruments, his controls, he asked, "And what do they make of us, Ken?"

Mayhew replied, "They think that we're gods, of course. They're frightened, and have every right to be, but are determined not to show it. . ." The psionic communications officer laughed briefly. "I admire their attitude towards gods in general, and towards us in particular. Superhuman, but not supernatural. Their deities are, essentially, no more than better than life-size men and women. . ."

"And no less," said Grimes. "And no less. . ."

It occurred to him that he, himself, would be regarded as a god by these aborigines. A sort of minor Zeus, perhaps—or not so minor. He regarded the prospect with a rather smug equanimity. He would not complain. After all, wasn't he a Commodore, a Master Astronaut *and* a Master Mariner? At long last he would be getting his just due.

He chuckled briefly to himself, then concentrated on landing the ship. He focused his attention on a spot to sunward of a great, quartzite boulder that was casting a long, black shadow over grass that was more brown than green. His sounding radar told him that the ground was solid enough to support the great weight of the ship. It was not quite level, but the tripedal landing gear was self-adjusting.

And there, plain in the screen, was a good target—a patch of grass that, for some reason, was more yellow than brown or green. Was it grass or was it a myriad of small flowers? The distinction was of no importance; Grimes applied a hint of lateral thrust and brought the natural beacon exactly into the center of the cartwheel sight. He was almost down. Altitude dropped from tens of meters to meters, then to less than a meter. The ship hung there for long seconds, her inertial drive grumbling to itself irritably. Slowly, slowly she settled. There was the slightest of jars, an almost undetectable rocking motion as the huge recoil cylinders of her landing gear took the shock, as her long axis maintained the vertical. The irregular beat of the

83

drive faded to a mutter. Yes, she was solid enough in the vaned tripod.

"Finished with engines," said the Commodore.

"Go an' see them?" asked Williams. "Or let them come to see us?"

"Mphm. . ." grunted Grimes. He looked at the screen, which was now depicting the village on which the big telescope had been trained. He watched the people. They were tall, well proportioned; their scanty clothing or lack of any clothing at all made this obvious. Blond hair predominated among both men and women, although a substantial minority of the villagers were darkly brunette. All the grown men were bearded. They stood there, men, women and children, in a loose group, staring at the shining tower that had fallen miraculously from the skies. Even the dogs— shaggy, wolflike beasts—were staring. The other domestic animals—sheep, were they, or goats?— were going about their business as usual.

The Commodore looked at them, feeling a certain envy. Here was the myth of the Noble Savage made flesh and blood. Here were people who were fitting ancestors to the Hellenes who later (how much later?) were to populate this land.

He said, prosaically, "How about getting some fresh air into this tin can, Commander?"

"Ay, ay, Skipper!" replied Williams, cheerfully. He used a telephone to give the necessary orders to the engineroom. Within seconds the fans were no longer circulating the spaceship's too many times used and re-used atmosphere but were drawing directly from outside. Somebody sneezed. The scent of pine trees was strong and mingled with it was a spicy, unidentifiable aroma.

At the village there was activity. People were going back into their huts and then reappearing. What would become a small procession was starting to assemble. There was a big man, taller than his fellows, who had put on crude body armor of leather, who was carrying a short, broad sword that gleamed like gold (that had to be bronze) in the morning sunlight. There were half a dozen other men, also armored, bearing flint-headed spears. There was a shambling giant—not as tall as the leader but much broader, heavily muscled— with the shaggy skin of some animal draped carelessly about his thick waist, the fur of it almost matching the hairiness of his own pelt. He was armed with a club, a roughly trimmed branch from a tree. And there were musicians—two pipers with primitive bagpipes, three drummers with skin-covered sections of hollowed-out log slung before their bodies. Their drumsticks—bones, they looked like—gleamed whitely.

Somebody in the control room extruded and switched on an exterior directional microphone. The rhythmic thud and rattle of the drums came beating in, and the thin, high skirling of the pipes. For the benefit of any among his people boasting Scottish ancestry, Grimes remarked that *that* music hadn't changed much over the centuries. Williams asked, "Are you *sure* this is Greece, Skipper?" "I can't see any kilts," contributed Carnaby, who was more interested in the women bringing up the rear of the procession than the men. "Not even a sporran. . ."

"Mphm," grunted Grimes, with a this-has-gone-far-enough intonation. With his officers he looked at the screen. The villagers were marching steadily towards the ship, led by the big, armored man and the skin-clad giant. They were followed by the musicians, behind whom were the spearmen. Bring-

ing up the rear came the women, naked, all of
them, moving with the grace that comes naturally
to those accustomed from childhood to carrying
burdens on their heads. And these women were so
burdened—with big jars, with baskets. One had the
carcass of some small animal, a kid or a lamb.

"Sacrifices?" Grimes asked Mayhew.

"No, Commodore. Not exactly. . . These are
awkward minds. . . They're transmitting, after a
fashion, but there doesn't seem to be a receiver
among the bunch of them. Sacrifices? Peace offerings, I'd say."

"An odd sort of reaction from a bunch of primi-
tives. . ."

"Not so odd, perhaps. They've yet to evolve a
theology, with all the trimmings. As I said before,
their gods, such as they are, are superhuman rather
than supernatural. . ."

"And I suppose I'd better go down to receive
these. . . peace offerings."

"I. . . I think so. . ."

Briefly Grimes pondered the advisability of
changing into dress uniform with its stiff linen,
frock coat, fore-and-aft hat and ceremonial sword.
But such regalia would be meaningless to these
people—and, besides, the air temperature outside the
ship was already twenty-five Centigrade degrees,
and rising. His shorts and shirt would have to do,
and his best cap with the scrambled egg on the
peak of it, the golden laurel leaves, still undimmed
by time. (And wasn't it in Greece where the laurel
wreath, as a mark of honor, first originated?)

He said to Williams, "All right, Commander.
Have the after airlock door opened, and the ramp
down." And to Hendriks, "Extrude your light armament to cover the immediate vicinity of the ship.
And I'm warning you, don't be trigger happy. Fire

only on direct orders from myself or Commander Williams." Finally, "I'd like a guard of honor, Major. Yourself and six of your most reliable men. Yes, wear your dress helmets, but with normal tropical khakis."

"And weapons?" asked Dalzell, adding "sir" as an afterthought.

"Mphm. Stunguns only."

"I'd suggest projectile pistols. Apart from its lethal qualities a fifteen-millimeter makes a nice loud bang."

"Stunguns only," repeated Grimes firmly. "*If* they are required, and *if* they aren't effective, Mr. Hendriks will be able to make enough noise with *his* toys to keep you happy."

The Major made no reply, saluted with deliberate sloppiness and stalked out of the control room. *Another unsatisfied customer. . .* thought Grimes. But the ruffled feelings of his Marines were the least of his worries.

He went down to his quarters to collect his cap. He watched Sonya as she changed from her short uniform skirt into sharply creased slacks. He said nothing, guessing that it was her reaction to the unashamed nudity of the native women. Like the majority of married men he had long since ceased to expect logical behavior from his wife.

"Ready?" he asked.

"Ready," she replied.

He led the way down to the after airlock.

Chapter 15

Slowly Grimes strode down the ramp, keeping step to the throb and rattle of the not-now-distant drums. The mad skirling of the approaching pipes was painful. He forced himself to ignore it. Sonya marched beside him, and Mayhew kept step a little to the rear. Behind them came Dalzell and his Marines, six of them, all big men. The drabness of their uniforms was obscured by the glitter of their accoutrements—the highly burnished brass, the medals with their rainbows of colored ribbons.

When he had rough, solid ground under his feet the Commodore halted. Sonya stood at his right hand, Mayhew at his left. Behind them stood Dalzell and his line of space soldiers. At the sight of these beings emerging from the ship the procession halted; the drums missed a beat or two, the pipers paused their shrill squealing. But the two big men in the van came steadily on, one holding his gleaming sword aloft, the other with his club carried casually over his shoulder. After their initial hesitation the others followed, but without the apparent arrogant confidence of their leaders.

Grimes stood his ground. He hoped that the Marines had their stun-guns ready.

No more than six feet from the spacemen the armored man came to a halt. The giant made another step and then shuffled clumsily backward to stand beside the other. The drums and (mercifully) the pipes fell silent. The spearmen and the gift-bearing women grouped themselves behind the others.

The Commodore stared impassively at the armored man—wearing, Sonya told him later, his best Admiral-Hornblower-on-the-quarterdeck expression. The native stared impassively at the Commodore. *And is it up to me*, Grimes asked himself, *to say, "Take me to your leader?" But he is the leader. Obviously*. The crude armor could not hide the superb proportions of his body. The bronze helmet and the bronze sword were conspicuous badges of rank.

And then the chief's sword hand moved. Sonya uttered a faint gasp. Dalzell snapped an order to his men. "Hold it!" whispered Mayhew urgently. "Hold it, Major!" And to Grimes, "It's all right, sir . . ."

The right hand, holding the sword, moved—but only to transfer the weapon to the left hand, which let it drop, holding it with the point down. The right hand, empty, was raised, palm out, in salute. Grimes responded, bringing the edge of his own right hand smartly to the peak of his cap. *And what now?* he wondered. *I suppose I graciously accept the gifts.*

"Not yet, sir," said Mayhew.

"Do they want to see first what we are going to give them?"

"No. It's rather more complicated. We have to prove our superiority."

"That shouldn't be hard," said Grimes, conscious of the towering bulk of his ship behind him, of the might of her weaponry. "In fact it should be obvious."

"I'm not so sure. . ." murmured Sonya. "I'm not so sure. . ." She was looking at the handsome figure of the chief with something like admiration. And then Grimes realized that it was not the chief at whom she was so looking; it was at the uncouth, shambling giant beside him.

"Mphm," grunted the Commodore dubiously.

The native leader said something in his own language. His voice was deep and musical, the words had a rhythm to them.

Mayhew murmured, "This is not an exact translation, but I'm picking up his thoughts as he speaks. Our champion will have to fight their champion."

Grimes looked at that big, bronze sword. Even now, held negligently in its owner's left hand, it appeared nastily lethal. He asked, "Can I use whatever weapon I wish? Do I have the choice of weapons?"

Mayhew replied, "It is not the king whom you have to fight, sir. He is not the champion on an occasion such as this. Herak, the man with the club, is the champion." He added, "And I think that it's supposed to be a fight with no weapons—or, to be exact, only with nature's weapons."

Relief dawned in the Commodore's mind. The king had his champion to do his fighting for him. What was good enough for a king was good enough for the captain of a ship. But . . . But could he *order* anybody to take on that hirsute hunk of overdeveloped muscle? The king of a savage community wields powers that, over the centuries, have been lost by mere shipmasters . . .

Dalzell stepped forward to talk with his superior. He said, "I think I get the drift of it, sir. You'll want a champion to beat the hell out of this Herak, or whatever he calls himself. Unless, of course, you'd sooner do it yourself . . ."

"I'm not an all-in wrestler, Major."

"I thought not, sir. But all of my men are well trained in unarmed combat. I could call for a volunteer . . ."

"Do that, Major."

The volunteer was Private Titanov—and he was a genuine volunteer. He stripped rapidly to his skimpy underpants. Divested of his uniform he could almost have been the twin of Herak. Herak grinned ferociously at him and he grinned back. It was as much a snarl as a grin. Herak handed his club to one of the spearmen, dropped the animal skin that was his only garment to the short grass, kicked it aside with a broad foot. It was picked up by a girl, who clasped it almost reverently to her full breasts. The giant flexed his muscles; they crawled under the hairy skin like thick snakes. He drummed on his barrel chest with his great fists, threw his head back and howled like a wolf.

Meanwhile, the king was giving orders in an authoritative voice. His people formed a rough ring, about ten meters in diameter, in the center of which the champion took his place. Herak grinned again and lifted his right arm; it was as thick as the thigh of a normal man. His fist was clenched. He did not need his heavy club. This was weapon enough.

The king looked towards Grimes. He said nothing, but the expression on his handsome, bearded face was easy enough to read. *Are you ready? Is your man ready?* "Yes," said the Commodore. "Yes." He hoped that the other would, somehow, understand him.

The king transferred his gleaming sword to his right hand, raised it, brought it down with a slashing motion. The drummers rattled briefly and noisily. The pipers emitted a short, strident squeal.

"Go, Titanov, go!" ordered Dalzell.

"Go, go, go!" chanted the other Marines.

Titanov went. He advanced slowly, crouching, massive shoulders hunched. He reached the perimeter of the ring. A man and a woman moved apart to allow him ingress. The woman detained him briefly, putting out her hand to finger, curiously, the material of his shorts. At least that is what Grimes, who had his prudish moments, hoped that she was doing. Titanov broke away, kept on coming. In spite of his bulk, his motion was like that of a great cat. His arms were hanging loosely at his sides, his fists were clenched. Not that this meant anything; a karate chop is deadlier than a punch. Then he was within range of Herak's right fist—which, suddenly, swept down like a steam hammer. Had it connected, the Marine's brains would have been spattered over the grass.

But it did not connect. Titanov skipped backwards with surprisingly delicate grace, like a ballet dancer—and he kicked, high, with deadly precision. Herak screamed, dreadfully and shrilly. He fell face forward on to the turf, clutching his genitals. His shoulders heaved as he noisily vomited.

Grimes heard Dalzell barking orders, realized that the Major feared that the foul fighting of his man might well precipitate hostile action on the part of the villagers. He grasped Sonya's arm, intending to spin her around and shove her towards the ramp at the first sign of trouble.

Mayhew laughed softly. "Don't worry, John. It was a fair fight as far as they are concerned. They accept the decision."

"More than I'd do in their shoes . . ."

"They're not wearing any."

The women had crowded around Titanov, embracing him, almost mobbing him. One of them had produced a wreath of green leaves from somewhere and had crowned him with it. Evidently the felled champion was not popular.

"Titanov!" snapped Dalzell. Then, in a louder voice, "Titanov!"

"Sir?" replied the Marine at last.

"Come back here and get dressed. At once!"

"Sir."

Titanov managed to extricate himself from his female admirers. They let him go reluctantly. He walked slowly back towards the ship. He had lost his underpants, but did not seem to be at all embarrassed.

Chapter 16

"And what now?" Grimes asked Mayhew. He looked with pity towards the groaning Herak, still huddled on the grass, now in a foetal position. He said, "Perhaps I should send for the Doctor to do what he can for that poor bastard . . ."

"No, sir. I advise against it. I have an idea that the local wise woman or witch or whatever will be out soon from the village to take care of him . . ."

"And what's the king saying?"

"He's ordering his women to present the gifts to you."

"Oh. And what do I do?"

"Accept them graciously. Smile. Say something nice. *You* know."

"Mphm. I think that can be managed. And do I reciprocate?"

"Only to the king, sir. His name, I think, is Hektor . . ."

"And what would he like?"

"He's rather hoping, sir, that you'll present him with something fancy in the way of weapons . . ."

"Firearms are out of the question," snapped Grimes testily. He was feeling out of his depth. On a normal survey voyage there would have been a horde of specialists to advise him—experts in linguistics, sociology, zoology, botany, geology . . . The list was almost endless. Now he had not so much as a single ethologist. He was lucky to have two excellent telepaths; their talent helped him to surmount, after a fashion, the language barrier.

"Your dress sword . . ." suggested Sonya. "I never did like that anachronistic wedding-cake cutter."

"*No.*"

"If I may make a suggestion, sir," said Dalzell, "my Artificer Sergeant has been amusing himself making some rather good arbalests—crossbows. He thought that such weapons could be useful if, at some time, we ran completely out of ammunition for our projectile rifles and pistols . . ."

"Thank you, Major. One of those should do very nicely . . ."

Dalzell spoke into his wrist-transceiver, then said to Grimes, "The arbalest will be down in a couple of seconds, sir."

"Good."

The king was approaching slowly, his gleaming sword once again held proudly aloft. Behind him marched the women with the jars and the baskets, the slaughtered lamb, balanced on their heads. They moved gracefully, their naked bodies swaying seductively as they walked. Some of them were blondes and some brunettes, and the skins of all of them were a lustrous, golden brown. Grimes—and the other men—watched them with undisguised admiration.

Sonya said sharply, "Beware the Greeks when they come bearing gifts!"

"Ha!" snorted Grimes. "Ha! Very funny."

"But rather apt, my dear."

The king stood to stiff attention, a little to one side of the line of advance of the gift-bearers. Slowly the leading woman, a statuesque blonde, approached Grimes. With both hands she lifted the jar from her head and then, falling to her knees with a fluid motion, deposited it on the grass at the commodore's feet. She got up, bowed, then turned and walked away.

"You didn't thank her," said Sonya. "But no doubt your mind was on other things, although not higher things . . ."

"I think that's oil in the jar," said Mayhew. "Olive oil."

Grimes was ready for the other women. As each of them made her presentation he smiled stiffly and murmured, "Thank you, thank you . . ." Some of the baskets, he saw, contained grain and others held berries. Probably, he thought, some of the jars would contain wine or beer. He began to wonder what it would be like . . .

"Sir, sir!" It was Dalzell's Artificer Sergeant. "The crossbow, sir."

"Oh, yes." Grimes took the weapon in his right hand. It was heavy, but not overly so. He examined it curiously and with admiration. There was a stirrup at the head wide enough to take even a big foot. For cocking it there was not a small windlass, as was used in the first arbalests, but an ingeniously contrived folding lever. The construction was metal throughout. Modern in design and manufacture as it was, it would never be the superb rapid-fire weapon that the longbow became (was to become) but it was powerful, and deadly, and accurate . . . The king had approached Grimes, was standing over him. Eager anticipation was easy to read in his bearded face.

"Would you mind demonstrating, Sergeant?" asked the commodore, handing the crossbow back to the man.

"Certainly, sir." The sergeant lowered the stirrup to the ground, put his right foot into it, then heaved upwards with both hands grasping the cocking lever, grunting with the effort. There was a sharp *click* as the pawl engaged. He then took a steel quarrel from the pouch at his belt, inserted it into the groove. He raised the skeleton butt to his shoulder. He kept it there, but looked puzzled. "What's me target, sir?" he asked.

The king guessed the meaning of the words even if he did not know the language in which they were spoken. He smiled broadly, pointed to the unfortunate Herak. The defeated wrestler had managed to sit up, was being attended to by a filthy old hag in a tattered skin robe who was holding a crude, clay cup of some brew to his lips.

The sergeant would have been quite capable of using this target—but, "No," ordered Grimes firmly. "*No.*"

"But I could shoot the mug outa her hands, sir . . ."

"You're not to try it. Use that!" *That* was a small, yellow-white boulder about two hundred meters distant.

"But it'll damage the quarrel, sir."

"That's too bad. Aim. Shoot!"

"Very good, sir," responded the man in a resigned voice.

The taut wire bowstring twanged musically. The

short, metal shaft flashed in the sunlight as it sped towards the rock. It hit in a brief, sudden explosion of glittering dust. And when this cleared the boulder was seen to be split in two; sheer good chance had guided the projectile to a hidden fault line.

The king rumbled obvious approval. He thrust his sword into the ground, held out both his big hands for the new toy. He took hold of it lovingly and then, with almost no fumbling, succeeded in cocking it. The sergeant handed him a bolt. Grimes moved as unobtrusively as possible so that his body was between the native ruler and what probably would be his choice of targets.

But there was a herd of goats drifting slowly over the grassy plain towards the ship. The king grinned again, took careful aim on the big, black buck in the lead. He seemed to be having a little trouble understanding the principle of the sights with which the weapon was fitted, but at last pulled the trigger.

It was another lucky shot, catching the hapless animal squarely in the head, between the horns.

What have I done? Grimes asked himself guiltily. But surely the bow was already in existence, and the introduction of the arbalest into this world, even though it might be a few centuries too early, would make very little difference to the course of history.

"We have a satisfied customer, sir," said Dalzell smugly.

"Mphm," grunted Grimes.

Chapter 17

After the exchange of gifts—the crossbow, a few knives, a couple of hammers and a saw for the baskets of produce and the jars of oil, beer and milk—the natives returned to their village. Grimes wondered if he and a party should accompany them, but Mayhew advised against it. "They wouldn't object, John; they're essentially too courteous. But the party's laid on for tonight, and they have to get things ready . . ."

"What party?" asked Grimes.

"Do you expect a gilt-edged invitation card?" Sonya asked him.

"I suppose not." He turned again to the telepath. "So there's to be a feast, is that it?"

"Yes. In our honor."

"Then the samples of the local foodstuffs will be useful. Major Dalzell, please have these gifts delivered to the Bio-Chemist, and tell him from me to go into a huddle with the Quack to find out if we can enjoy the wine and food of the country without serious consequences . . ."

"Yes, sir."

"And, Major . . ."

"Sir?"

"There is to be no, repeat no, fraternizing with the natives. I shall give the same order to Commander Williams regarding the spacemen and -women of the ship's complement."

"Understood, sir."

Grimes could not help noticing the expressions on the faces of Dalzell's Marines. If looks could have killed, he would have had only another second to live. Titanov glowered even more ferociously than his mates.

"And what about tonight's . . . er . . . feast?" asked the Major.

"I'll let you know later," said Grimes. He heard one of the men mutter, "One o' those officers-only bun struggles, I suppose . . ." But it would not be, he had already decided. It would all too probably be the sort of affair at which any staid, respectable senior officer should be conspicuous by his absence.

Back aboard the ship Grimes called Williams, Mayhew and Clarisse into his quarters. He said, "We know *where* we are. We still don't know *when*."

"Wasn't there a Bronze Age?" asked Williams. "The sword that the chief or king or whatever he is was carrying looked like bronze . . ."

"An Age is an Age is an Age," remarked Sonya. "In other words, it's not a mere two or three weeks."

Grimes grunted irritably. His wife was right, as she usually was. The Bronze Age, following the Stone Age, had lasted for quite a while. But when, roughly, had it started? He, Grimes, did not know, and he doubted very much if anybody in the ship knew. *Faraway Quest's* data banks were stuffed almost to bursting with information on just about everything but ancient Terran history.

"This period," said Sonya, "must be towards the beginning of the Bronze Age . . ."

"How do you make that out?" asked Williams.

"Metal artifacts are so scarce as to be the perquisites of the rulers. The local king has a bronze sword. The spears of his soldiers are tipped with stone."

"Could be," admitted Grimes. "Could be. On the other hand, this may be a backward, poverty-stricken little kingdom. Just as in *our* day and age not every world can afford the very latest in sophisticated weaponry."

"There are precious few planets that can't," she told him. "Guns before butter has been a working principle of Man for all the millennia that he has been Man. It was a working principle ages before that mad German dictator—Hitler, wasn't it?—coined the phrase."

"So we can assume," said the commodore, "that bronze artifacts are rare as well as being expensive."

"You can assume all you like, my dear, but that does seem to be the way of it."

"Mphm. 2,000 B.C.? 3,000? I read up on Greek history after I got involved in that Spartan Planet affair, but I'm afraid that not much of it stuck in my memory. In any case, I never could remember dates. This land, as I recall it, was settled by a variety of peoples, some coming by sea and some by land. Our friends in the village seem to be land nomads who have settled down in one spot, who are living in permanent wooden houses rather than

101

tents. But they should have horses, and we haven't seen any . . ."

"Horses," said Sonya, "have been known to die. Perhaps some epidemic in the past wiped all their horses out, so they had to stay put and make the best of it."

"But they should have cattle," persisted Grimes.

"Not necessarily. They have sheep, and goats . . ."

"And figs," added Williams. "And some very small pears . . ."

"How do you know?"

"I looked in the baskets when the pongoes brought them aboard."

"I hope," said Sonya, "that you did no more than look."

"I was tempted," admitted the commander. "But I've no desire to come down with a case of the squitters. I hope that the local tucker *is* passed fit for human—our sort of human—consumption."

"Yes," said Grimes, "I do, too. We have this feast tonight. Have you any idea, Ken, what's being laid on for us?"

"It'll be a barbecue," answered the telepath. "Already they're slaughtering lambs and kids . . ."

"Sounds a bit of all right," commented Williams, licking his lips.

"I'm sorry, Billy," Grimes told him, "but you won't be among the guests."

"Have a heart, Skipper!"

"I'm sorry, and I mean it. But somebody has to watch the shop. I shall require a skeleton crew remaining on board—you, in command in my absence, and Hendriks, in case any show of force is required, and either the Chief or the Second Engineer . . . And such ratings as you consider necessary."

"Talking of the engineers—the Chief wants to

have a grand overhaul of the inertial drive. He was telling me that it'll not be safe to lift off until he's satisfied himself that everything is as it should be."

"We'll see how things go tonight," said Grimes. "If I'm reasonably happy he can take things apart tomorrow. Meanwhile, arrange a meeting of all hands for 1600 hours."

Faraway Quest's people were in a restive mood when they assembled in the Main Lounge at 1600 hrs. This was understandable. Outside the ship there was an unspoiled world, bathed in sunshine. Inside the ship there were the same old drab surroundings, and the subtle scents of thyme and asphodel, mingled with the aroma of distant pines, drifting through the ventilation system, made their virtual imprisonment harder to endure.

However, Grimes, when he mounted his platform, had the attention of the meeting.

He opened proceedings briefly, then said, "You will all be pleased to learn that the samples of foodstuffs and liquor brought on board have been passed as fit for human consumption. It will be necessary, however, for all hands to receive a broad spectrum anti-biotic injection to ensure their continuing good health while on this world. This will also lessen the possibility of our transmitting any diseases to the natives, although after our long spell in Space we should be practically sterile." He smiled briefly. "In the surgical sense of the word, of course. Mphm.

"As many of you are already aware there will be a feast in the village tonight. I am given to understand that we shall be the honored guests. Save for a shipkeeping skeleton crew—the duty list will be posted by Commander Williams—we shall all attend. Rig of the day—of the evening, rather—will be

Number Seven. Major Dalzell will see to it that his men wear the Marine equivalent. Side-arms will be worn only by officers of Lieutenant Commander's rank and up, although Marine other ranks will carry stun-clubs. Weapons, however, are not, repeat not, to be used unless in circumstances of extreme provocation.

"All hands attending the feast will behave in a gentlemanly . . ." he grinned . . . "or ladylike manner. Remember that we are ambassadors. Do not partake too freely of the local liquor—or, if you do, do not fail to counteract the effects with anti-drunk tablets that you will all be carrying. Do *not* molest the native women. And as for you, ladies, try to avoid too close contact with the native men.

"And do not forget that even though you are away from the ship you are still subject to discipline.

"That is all."

He heard somebody mutter, "With old Pickle Puss keeping an eye on us it's going to be a fine party. I don't bloody think!"

Chapter 18

The sun was well down and the silvery sliver of the new moon, swimming in the afterglow, was about to lose itself behind the black peaks to the west'ard when the invitation to the feast was delivered. From the village marched a small procession—six men bearing aloft flaring, pine-knot torches, four drummers, two pipers. All of them were wrapped in cloaks of sheepskin against the evening chill. They paraded around the ship to the squealing of their pipes and the rattle of their drums.

Said Grimes sourly, "It *could* be a serenade . . ."

Mayhew told him, "I'm picking up their thoughts. It's a traditional melody, John. It could be called *Come To The Party* . . ."

"To be played on the typewriter?" asked Sonya. Then, "Now is the time for all good men to come to the party."

"And can we take our quick red foxes and lazy brown dogs with us?" wondered Grimes aloud. He got up out of his chair, reached for and put on his third-best uniform cap. He was wearing Number Seven uniform—tunic and trousers of tough khaki drill over a thick black sweater, black knee boots. It was the standard wear for shore excursions in rough country in less than subtropical temperature. For an occasion such as this promised to be the cloth had the big advantage of being stain-resistant.

Before leaving his quarters he said to Williams, "I don't anticipate any trouble, Billy. But if there is, we'll yell for help on our personal transceivers."

"I'll be listening, Skipper. Have a good time."

The commodore led the way down to the after airlock, followed by Sonya, Mayhew and Clarisse. The others were assembling there—ship's officers and ratings, Dalzell and his Marines. They stood to one side to allow Grimes to be first down the ramp.

As he stepped on to the ground the torch bearers advanced and then, with their flambeaux, made a beckoning gesture. They turned about and, flanked by the pipers and the drummers, began to march back towards the village. The commodore and his party fell in behind them, then a larger contingent of men and women led by Carnaby, finally the major and his men.

It was rough going in the deepening dusk; the fitful flare of the torches was more of a nuisance than a help. Luckily most of the boulders were well clear of the short grass and glimmered whitely. Nonetheless, Grimes was thankful for his stout boots.

On they marched to the barbaric music, towards the dark huddle of houses among which fires flared and flickered ruddily. Downwind drifted the tang of wood smoke, the aroma of roasting meat. Grimes realized that he was starting to salivate. Nobody could have described *Faraway Quest* as a

THE WAY BACK

hungry ship—but tank-grown food loses, after a very few weeks, its essential flavors, its individuality.

Suddenly drummers and pipers fell silent, but there was still music. They were singing in the village, a song in which male and female voices blended in compulsive rhythm.

"And what is that?" Grimes asked Mayhew.

"A . . . a welcome . . ." The telepath tripped over a rock and would have fallen flat on his face had Clarisse not caught him. "A welcome reserved for heroes or for superior beings . . ."

"Gods?" asked Grimes.

"As I keep saying," replied Mayhew, "these people regard gods as sort of older brothers. Powerful, but not quite omnipotent, and with all sorts of all-too-human weaknesses . . ."

"That last part is true as far as we're concerned!"

They were very close to the village now. The low houses stood in black silhouette against the glare of the fires—which must be, Grimes decided, in some sort of central square. The noise of singing was loud. And then he saw a huge figure, dark against the unsteady firelight, advancing to meet them. The torch bearers and the musicians stepped to one side to make way for the newcomer. It was the king, Hektor. In one hand he held not his sword but the arbalest, in the other a huge mug. He thrust this at Grimes, who had to use both his hands to grasp it.

"Drink it. All of it," urged Mayhew in a whisper.

The commodore lifted the vessel to his lips. He toasted briefly, "Down the hatch!" He sipped—then decided ruefully that this was something he would have to get over with quickly. He liked beer, and this was beer, but . . . It smelled musty and tasted

107

mustier. It had an unpleasantly thick consistency, and there were semi-solid bodies suspended in it.

He gulped and swallowed manfully.

He muttered, "Garrgh!"

But he finished the muck in one draught. At least, it was alcoholic . . .

The king was leading the way now to where the feast was already in progress. It was, decided Grimes, quite a party. There were at least six huge fires burning in the village square; two of them were blazing, affording illumination, the other four were beds of red coals over which the spitted carcasses of animals dripped and sizzled, spurts of yellow flame marking the fall of each spatter of hot fat. The older women were attending to the cookery; the younger ones came dancing out to meet the party from the ship. A trio of beauties, more naked than otherwise, surrounded the commodore, and one of them hung a garland of rather wilted flowers about his neck.

"And which one are you giving the apple to?" whispered Sonya.

But these were no pale-skinned animated statues. These were shapely girls, very human, whose sun-browned skins gleamed ruddily in the firelight. The blonde who had presented the garland, greatly daring, threw her slim yet strong arms around Grimes' shoulders, brought her face close to his in a gesture of invitation. He hesitated only for a second, then kissed her full on the mouth. Her lips were greasy; it was obvious that she had been sampling one of the roasts of lamb—but, Grimes told himself, they tasted far better than that vile beer had and were just as intoxicating.

"Down, boy, down!" growled Sonya.

Reluctantly the commodore disengaged the girl's arms from his neck, put his own hands on her shoulders and turned her away from him. He could not resist the temptation to speed her on her way with a friendly slap on the buttocks. She squealed happily.

They were led by the villagers to places around the fire—Grimes and his party, Carnaby and the men and women with him, Dalzell and his Marines. They sat on the threadbare grass, not too comfortably, yet pleasantly conscious of the heat from the flames. Men and women brought them mugs of drink. The commodore sipped his dubiously, but it was wine this time, much too sweet but a vast improvement on the beer. And there was coarse bread in thin, flat cakes, and rough hunks of hot meat, lamb and kid, thyme- and onion- and garlic-flavored. There was the continual drumming, and the singing, and—almost inaudible in the general uproar—the squealing of the pipes.

There was dancing.

There was a circle of girls weaving sinuously about a huge, naked, bearlike man crowned with a wreath of green leaves, laughing shrilly as he reached out and tried to grab them. It must be Herak, Grimes thought at first, and was pleased that the defeated wrestler had made a good recovery. Herak? No, it was the Marine, Titanov.

He nudged Sonya.

"Do you see what I see?"

"What of it?" she countered.

"He . . . He's going native . . ." And he thought, *This won't do at all, at all. Have to put a stop to it . . .* He realized that his thinking was getting muzzy, fumbled for the no-drunk tablets in his pocket, swallowed two of them.

He got unsteadily to his feet, walked with careful deliberation to where Dalzell was reclining on the grass like a dissolute Roman, attended closely

by two women. One of them was feeding him with
bite-sized pieces that she was tearing from a leg of
lamb, the other was holding a mug to his lips at
frequent intervals.

"Major!"

"Commodore . . ."

"That man of yours. The wrestler . . ."

"What man? Where?"

"There . . ."

But as Grimes pointed he realized that Titanov
was gone—and with him, presumably, had gone the
dancing girls. But there was a little heap of uniform
clothing not far from Dalzell, and a stunclub was
on top of the garments.

"What about *that*?"

"The fire's hot, Commodore. Thinkin' of gettin'
stripped off myself . . ."

"But . . ."

But the fire *was* hot, and it was bloody absurd
wearing this heavy khaki . . . Grimes had unbut-
toned his jacket when his ears were assailed by a
strident blast of music. He turned to look at its
source. One part of his mind was horrified—another, almost as strong, part accepted what he saw
as being right and proper. Strutting by came one of
his stewardesses. He remembered her name, Maggie
Macpherson. She was wearing nothing but her
kneeboots and jauntily angled forage cap, and she
was playing a set of the native bagpipes, and playing them as well as such instruments can ever be
played. He even recognized the tune, the traditional *Scotland The Brave*. After her pranced a
small procession—three of her fellow stewardesses, a
quartet of junior engineers, a half dozen villagers,
three of whom were children.

He thrust out a detaining hand. "Miss Macpherson!"

The music squealed to a dying-pig finish.

"Miss Macpherson, what is the meaning of this?"

"What is the meaning of what, sir?"

"You . . . You aren't properly dressed . . ."

"I'm wearin' me cap, sir . . ."

"Gie us *The Scottish Soldier*, Maggie!" shouted one of the engineers.

"John!" It was Mayhew, his voice urgent.

"What is it, Ken?"

Grimes could not hear the telepath's reply for the renewed skirling of the pipes.

"Speak up, man!"

"It's the wine, John," almost shouted Mayhew. "Not the same wine as we had analyzed. Something in it. Mushrooms, I think . . ."

"Could be . . ." muttered the commodore. Whatever it was, the drug was converting what had been a feast—a rather rough one, admittedly—into an orgy. The scene illuminated by the fitful flaring of the fires could have been painted by Hieronymus Bosch. And yet Grimes was feeling revulsion only because he thought that he *should* be feeling revulsion. But as long as he kept his uniform on, that part of his personality which he regarded as "the commodore" would remain in the ascendancy.

He demanded, "Can you and Clarisse control my people?"

"It's all we can do to keep ourselves in control . . . Carnaby is still more or less in possession of his senses, and Brenda Cole . . . Apart from them . . . But you must *do* something, John. There're our weapons lying around for anybody to pick up . . ."

And where the hell was Sonya? Grimes looked around for her, but could not see her. Accompanied by Mayhew, he hurried back to where he had left her. Her jacket was on the grass, and her slacks, her belt with the holstered pistol—and, beside them, what looked like a wolfskin breech-clout and something that gleamed metalically. It was the steel arbalest.

But he, Grimes, was responsible for the entire ship's company, not just for one woman, even though she was his wife. (And, he knew very well, she was quite capable of looking after herself.) First of all he would have to put a stop to this . . . this orgy, and then there would be some sorting out.

He raised his wrist transceiver to his mouth.

"Commodore to *Quest*. Commodore to Commander Williams. Do you read me? Over."

It was a woman's voice that answered. Grimes remembered that Ruth Macoboy, the Assistant Electronic Communications Officer, was among Williams' shipkeepers.

"*Quest* here, Commodore. Bill—Commander Williams, I mean—is coming to the transceiver now."

"Williams here, Skipper. Anything wrong?"

"Plenty, Bill. First of all, get Hendriks to plaster the village with Morpheus D. Don't open fire, though, until I give the word. We shall be getting away from the place as soon as we can. Send somebody from the ship to meet us with half a dozen respirators. Got that?"

"Have got, Skipper. Hendriks can load his pop-guns, but he's not to fire until you say so."

"Correct. We're on the way out now."

Clarisse appeared with Carnaby and Brenda Coles in tow. They seemed to be sober enough, but rather resentful. And then, to Grimes' surprise and great relief, Sonya came running up to them, her legs indecently long and graceful under the black sweater. She gasped, "That . . . lout!"

"Never mind him. Out of here. Fast."

"But . . . My clothes . . ."

"Come *on*, damn you!" Grimes grabbed his wife by the arm, hurried her out of the village.

Behind them somebody was wordlessly shouting, the bellowing of a frustrated animal. Then something whirred between Grimes and Sonya, narrowly missing both of them. A quarrel, the commodore realized, a bolt from Hektor's arbalest. There was a second missile—another very near miss—and a third.

"Down!" ordered Grimes, suiting the action to the word. He spoke into his wrist transceiver, "Commodore to *Quest*. Fire!"

From the fighting top of the distant ship came a flickering of pale flame and then, after what seemed a long interval, a series of sharp reports. The projectiles from Hendriks' guns wailed overhead and, almost immediately, came the dull thuds as the gas shells burst precisely over the village. Grimes could visualize that heavy, soporific vapour settling, oozing downwards through the air, permeating every building, every nook and cranny.

Abruptly the wild singing and the shouting died and the drums fell silent.

But a lone piper—was it Maggie Macpherson? It had to be—persisted for long minutes, an eldritch lament that blended perfectly with the thin, cold drizzle that was beginning to fall.

But even she must, in the end, inhale, and then there was complete silence.

113

Chapter 19

Williams came out from the ship in one of the work boats, a flying craft that was little more than a platform fitted with a powerful inertial drive unit. He was using his searchlight, and Grimes and the others stood up and waved as he drifted towards them. He brought the ungainly thing down to a soft landing a meter or so from where they were waiting, then asked, "What the hell's been happening, Skipper?"

The commodore found it hard to reply. He was almost overcome by a lethargy far deeper than that resulting from overindulgence in alcohol. But, with a great effort, he forced himself to reply. He finished, "And things were . . . getting out of hand. Only one thing to do . . . Put everybody to sleep . . ."

"Sure you didn't get any o' the gas yourself, Skipper? You sound pretty dopey to me."

"It was . . . the drug."

"So you think you were all drugged?"

"*Think?*" snapped Grimes testily. "I *know* we were drugged." He remembered vividly the taste and the smell of that beer-like drink, its consistency. Lucky he hadn't liked it, had downed only one mug of the muck. A concoction brewed from sacred mushrooms for special occasions? That assumption made sense.

"And what do we do now, Skipper?"

Grimes pulled himself together, gave orders. He and the others put on respirators, clambered aboard the work boat. Williams restarted the drive then cruised slowly, at low altitude, towards the village. The engine was horridly noisy in the quiet night, but nobody would hear it; the effects of the Morpheus D would take at least six hours to wear off. The fires were still burning in the village square but they were now little more than mounds of red embers, and in the glare of the searchlight no more than grey cinders. Grimes looked down and ahead anxiously; he was suddenly afraid that some of the anaesthetized revellers might have fallen into the beds of red-hot coals. But nobody had done so. The tangles of limbs and bodies were all well clear of danger.

Williams landed the raft in a narrow lane just away from the square. Grimes, followed by the rest of the party, jumped down to the ground. The drizzle had misted his goggles and he doubted if he would be able to tell, even with the aid of the powerful hand torch that Williams had given him, who were members of his own crew and who were natives. Nudity makes for anonymity.

The first body he came to was that of Maggie Macpherson. There was no mistaking her for anybody else. She still had the bagpipes, clasping the instrument to her breasts. It looked as though she were giving suck to some bloated little arthropoidal monster. Her uniform cap was, somehow, still on her unruly red curls. She still had her boots on. Grimes laughed—not an easy action to perform while wearing a respirator, but possible. This could be simple after all, so long as the others had shown the same respect for uniform regulations as had the Scottish girl.

And so it turned out to be, although some of the tangles took some sorting out. *Faraway Quest's* crew hadn't died with their boots on—but they had been doing all sorts of other things when the anesthetic gas hit them. At one stage Williams muttered, "I should have brought a camera . . . What a marvelous picture this would make! Twelve people in six poses . . ."

"Pipe down and get on with the bloody job!" growled Grimes. "It's quite bad enough without your making a joke of it!"

But it was Williams who knew how many bodies to look for and who kept a tally of those piled aboard the raft. It was Williams who said that Titanov was still missing, and who over-rode his superior's suggestion that the Marine be left to stew in his own juice. The big man was found at last, in one of the houses. An untidy heap of six naked girls had to be lifted off him before his body could be carried outside.

Another tally was made—of the weapons that had been recovered. Officers' side arms and the Marines' stunclubs were loaded aboard the workboat, together with a pile of discarded clothing. From this latter Sonya recovered her own uniform, got into it hastily.

Then, "We have to find the king," said Grimes.

"Why?" asked Williams.

"Because the bastard shot at us. I'm taking back his crossbow."

116

THE WAY BACK

Carrying torches, the two men walked slowly through the sleeping village. For what seemed a long time they searched in vain. At last their lights showed two giant, huddled bodies, were reflected from gleaming steel.

One of the unmoving men was Hektor, and he was dead, his skull messily crushed. The other was Herak, with the crossbow, which he had used as a club, still in his hands.

The king was dead—and who would be the next king?

That, Grimes told himself, was no concern of his.

Chapter 20

It was a long night, and a wearing one, and Grimes was still feeling muzzy from the effects of the mushroom beer. So was Sonya, and so were Carnaby and Brenda Coles, although the Navigator and the Assistant Biochemist had done little more than to take experimental sips of the stuff. Williams, of course, was exhibiting the infuriating, cheerful competency of the virtuously sober—but if it had not been for his efforts the sleeping crew members would never have been tucked away in their own quarters before daylight. Even so, the flush of dawn was bright in the east when the job was finally over.

Grimes turned in all standing, taking off only his jacket and his boots. He did not sleep in his bedroom—relations between him and Sonya were, naturally, rather strained, although it seemed doubtful if the late king had actually *done* anything—but on the settee in his day cabin. As his head touched the cushion he was using as a pillow he went out like a light.

When he woke up it was as though somebody had switched that figurative light back on. He was suddenly aware that someone was standing over him. He opened his eyes, realized that he was looking almost directly into the muzzle of a large-caliber projectile pistol. At this close range it was like the business end of a forty-millimeter cannon.

Behind the gun, he realized eventually, was Dalzell, who was grinning wolfishly.

"Major!" demanded Grimes. "What is the meaning of this?"

"Not Major, Commodore," replied the Marine. "Not any longer. You will address me as Your Majesty."

He must have had a skinful, thought Grimes. *He's still hallucinating like a bastard . . . I shall have to be tactful . . .* He said, "Would you mind putting that thing down?"

"Your Majesty," prompted Dalzell. "Yes, I would mind. And get this into your stupid skull—from now on *I* give the orders."

This was too much. "Have you gone mad?" roared Grimes.

"No, Commodore. Just a sudden rush of sanity to the head. That mushroom beer or whatever it was last night cleared my brain. I am seeing things in their proper perspective. What the hell's the use of beetling all around the Galaxy, not even knowing what we're looking for, when there's a kingdom—the nucleus of an empire—right here and now, just for the picking up?"

"I still say that you're mad."

"Careful, Commodore. Or Mr. ex-Commodore. I hold the ship."

"*You?* You're not a spaceman."

119

"I have the military power. And Hendriks is with me—he's a Master Astronaut, for what that's worth, as well as being the Gunnery Officer. And Sparks. And the engineers. And the Quack, and all the tabbies . . ." He laughed at the alarm that must have shown on Grimes' face. "No need to get too worried—yet. We haven't killed any of your pets. We might still find a use for them."

"My . . . pets?"

"The two tame telepaths. Williams. Carnaby. Their popsies."

"Their . . . popsies?"

"Really, Commodore. You surprise me. Your own ship—although not any longer!—and you don't know all that's going on aboard her. Ruth Macoboy and Brenda Coles, that's who. Williams and Carnaby are loyal to *you*—the Odd Gods of the Galaxy alone know why!—and the two wenches are loyal to their boyfriends. It's as simple as that."

Grimes watched the pistol hopefully, but with all the time that Dalzell was talking, it did not waver so much as a fraction of a degree.

Then— "What's simple?" asked Sonya coldly. She was standing in the doorway to the bedroom, dressed still in her black sweater and khaki trousers, holding Grimes' Minetti. The deadly little automatic was pointing straight at the Major.

Dalzell laughed. He remarked in a very reasonable voice, "If you pull *your* trigger, Mrs. Grimes—or, if you like, Commander Verrill—reflex action will cause me to pull mine. Not that it much matters as, in any case, your everloving husband will get his fair share of the burst intended for me. Furthermore . . ." He pursed his lips and whistled softly. Grimes did not have to turn his head to see that two Marines had entered his day cabin.

"So . . ." murmured Sonya regretfully.

"So drop your gun, Mrs. Grimes. Or Commander Verrill. Better make it Mrs. Grimes. A Commander's commission in the Terran Survey Service doesn't pile on many G's here and now, does it?"

"Better do as the man says," muttered Grimes at last.

"As the *man* says? You forget yourself, Commodore. As the *king* says."

"The Major has promoted himself," explained Grimes mildly.

Surprisingly Dalzell took this in good part. He grinned, then said, "There was a vacancy, and I applied for the job. I displayed my qualifications—noisy ones, and quite spectacular . . ." His face hardened, took on a vicious twist. "On your feet, Commodore! I've wasted too much time yapping to you. My men will escort you to the empty storeroom we're using as a brig."

"I shall need . . ." began Sonya.

"You need nothing. You'll get food and water, and there's a disposal chute for your personal wastes. Shake the lead out of your pants, the pair of you!"

Grimes sighed. A man and a woman, unarmed, against at least three armed men, all of whom were trained fighters. He almost wished that Sonya had used her pistol, disastrous as the results would have been. Now the weapon was on the deck, out of reach.

"All right," he said, rolling off the settee. "All right."

Grimes and Sonya made their slow way down through the ship. Save for their escort they saw nobody. Were the crew members avoiding him of their own volition or had they been ordered so to

121

do by Dalzell? Not that it mattered. The Major, judging from his attitude, was very firmly in the saddle.

They came at last to the storeroom, one of those on the farm deck. It was ideal for its purpose—that of a jail cell—as it was more of a utility compartment than a storeroom proper, and had been used as a handling room for meat from the tissue-culture vats. There were benches, and washing facilities. Even with six people in it there was no overcrowding. The other four were Williams, Carnaby, Ruth Macoboy and Brenda Cole. The Commander's rugged face was badly battered. He, at least, had put up a fight. He growled sardonically as the Commodore and Sonya were thrust into the prison, "Welcome aboard, Skipper. This is Liberty Hall; you can spit on the mat and call the cat a bastard!"

Grimes ignored this. "Where are Ken and Clarisse?" he demanded.

"Stashed away somewhere else, I reckon. They musta been pounced on first, so that they couldn't warn us. Not that they could have warned us about Dalzell an' his bloody pongoes, thanks to that fancy anti-telepathic conditioning of theirs."

"But the others. The real crew members. Ken must have had some warning, surely. A mutiny doesn't just happen, out of thin air."

"Gotta be a first time for anything, Skipper—an' this it. Don't forget that all of you were as high as kites on that fancy mushroom juice. Could be, too, that the muck damped out Ken's talents rather than enhancing 'em. But Ken an' Clarisse ain't here, that's for certain. Which is a bloody pity. If they were, we might cook somethin' up between us . . ."

And they can "hear" us, thought Grimes, *but we can't "hear" them. I could suggest that they teleport themselves here, but unless Clarisse has*

122

sketching materials to hand—which she won't have;
Dalzell's no fool—there's no way at all that it can
be done . . . There was a faint dawning of hope.
But isn't there? Grimes had read of prisoners using
their body wastes, their blood even, to write or
draw or paint.

A vivid picture formed itself in his mind. Wherever they were, the two telepaths were not very far
away and, with a pooling of powers and a great ex-
penditure of psionic effort, transmission of a sort
would be possible to the brains of non-telepaths.
Had they been in the same cell as Grimes it would
have been relatively easy, of course—but not, in
those circumstances, necessary.

Grimes, then, saw quite clearly the interior of a
storeroom not unlike the one in which he was imprisoned. There were two benches, on each of
which was a mattress. On one of the benches Mayhew was stretched supine, on the other one was
Clarisse. Each of them was secured firmly to his
bed by manacles at wrists and ankles.

And Clarisse could function as a teleporteuse
only when she was able to paint the people to be
moved or the locations to which they were to be
shifted.

Chapter 21

They must have been in their prison for all of three weeks.

They had no means of telling time; Dalzell had seen to it that they were stripped of any and all personal possessions of use or value, including their wristwatches. Meals came at irregular intervals. There was enough to sustain life, but with very little surplus. And always the food consisted of sandwiches so that there were never any table utensils that might be used as tools or weapons—not that knives or forks would have been any good against the machine pistols carried by the guards.

Time dragged.

Grimes grew a beard. He could not see it—there were, of course, no mirrors—but had to take Sonya's word for it that it was not becoming. Williams grew a beard, and it suited him. Carnaby was one of those who had undergone permanent depilation.

Sonya, although she tried very hard to maintain

appearances, lost her elegance. Brenda Coles, never very elegant to start with, lost weight. Ruth Macoboy, skinny rather than slim at all times, began, with her long, unkempt black hair to look like a fairy-tale witch. The tempers of the women soured as their appearance deteriorated.

Especially trying was the lack of privacy. At first, jokes were made about it, but, as the days wore on it became no laughing matter.

Meanwhile, what was happening?

Insofar as the ship was concerned, some not-too-far-off-the-beam guesswork was possible. It seemed obvious that Davis, the Chief Engineer, was striking troubles with the overhaul of the inertial drive unit. This would have taken no time at all had there been shoreside workshop facilities available—but here, of course, such were nonexistent. Through decks and bulkheads, all day and every day, drifted the noise of spasmodic hammering, but never the irregular beat that would tell of a test running of the engines.

And outside the ship?

Now and again Mayhew and Clarisse would succeed in transmitting a telepathic picture of events to Grimes, a relay of a picture which they, themselves, had picked up from some member of a shore party. The commodore watched, with helpless horror, what seemed to be an execution in the main square of the village—three white-bearded old men against a wall, a firing squad of Dalzell's Marines. Laser rifles were used, set at medium beam to ensure a spectacular incineration. Grimes watched, too, as those same Marines dragged six girls out of a house, carried them away somewhere out of the sight of the original viewer. Again he was horrified—then realized with disgust that the young women were putting up only a token resistance.

Dalzell figured, too, in these waking visions. Every time that the Major appeared he was wearing dress uniform, but with something that looked more like a crown than a helmet on his head. Some of the time he was supervising the building of what had to be a new palace—three-storied and with a sort of steeple to give it additional height, towering high over all the other houses in the village, including that which had been occupied by Hektor. At other times he was drilling his army—the Marines and also a sizeable force of young native men. These latter now had spears tipped with metal instead of obsidian, and short swords that gleamed like steel. That persistent hammering, Grimes decided, was probably not entirely due to the engine overhaul. Some of the engineers must be working as armament artificers.

Grimes was not the only one to pick up the psionic broadcasts made by Mayhew and Clarisse. Sonya shared them, as did Williams. Carnaby, Ruth Macoboy and Brenda Coles did not, but listened intently to what the others told them.

"That bloody pongo!" swore Williams, "is having himself one hell of a good time!"

"We most certainly are not," stated Sonya.

"But what does he intend to do with us?" asked Carnaby, of nobody in particular. Then, to Grimes, "You've made a study of this sort of thing, sir. Piracy, mutiny and all the rest of it. In the old days, I mean. At sea."

"I suppose I have, James," admitted the commodore.

"What usually happened to the victims of mutiny or piracy?" The young man looked as though he regretted having asked the question, but persisted with it. "What usually happened?"

Grimes had already given the matter considerable thought. He said, "It varied. It all depended on how bad a bastard the pirate captain or the leader of the mutineers was, and on how bad his men were. Some victims were made to walk the plank—which was not as funny as it sounds. It must have been a rather nasty method of execution. Some were marooned, on desert islands. Some—like Bligh of the *Bounty*—were cast adrift in open boats ..."

"*They* had a chance ..." muttered Carnaby.

"After this prison," remarked Sonya, "a desert island would seem like paradise."

"Depending, of course," Grimes told her, "on its location and on its natural resources. Here, we are sheltered from the weather and are getting adequate food."

"A defeatist attitude, John."

"Mphm. Perhaps. Don't forget that many a person has wished himself out of the frying pan and found himself in the fire."

"But Dalzell must have *some* intentions as far as we're concerned," persisted Sonya.

"But are they good ones?" asked Williams.

Probably not, thought Grimes. *Almost certainly not*. A thought insinuated itself into his mind—from outside was it? put there by Mayhew or Clarisse? A public trial, followed by a public execution ... Would Dalzell dare? Perhaps the major would consider a trial too risky, but the execution would make it plain to all hands that *he* now was the leader.

"And were you thinking what I was thinking?" asked Sonya.

"Yes."

"Me too," growled Williams.

127

"Did . . . did you receive something?" asked Brenda Coles.

"I'm not sure," Grimes told her. "I think we did." He tried to grin. "I think that Dalzell will turn out to be one of the really bad bastards."

"An' that brings me," put in Williams, "to something that I've been wanting to say for a long time. He, the major, has to do something about the Skipper and Sonya and meself. He can't afford to have us running around loose. But there's no reason at all why young James an' Brenda an' Ruth should be for the high jump. Next time that the pongoes bring us our tucker we can ask 'em to tell Dalzell that the three of you are willing to be faithful and loyal servants of his Majesty. You all have skills that he'll be needing."

"No," said Carnaby.

"*No*," said the two girls.

"If you have any sense," Grimes told them, "you'll say 'yes.' "

"*No!*" they told him. And they refused to be persuaded.

It was some hours later when the door to the storeroom opened.

And about time, thought Grimes irritably. The next meal wasn't due; it was considerably overdue. Even those unappetizing sandwiches would be welcome.

But no packets of sandwiches were tossed in through the barely opened door, which remained open. Grimes got to his feet, feeling the beginnings of hope. *Release*? Then his brief elation faded. This could only be a squad of Marines to lead him and the others to their execution.

"All right," he said. "Let's get it over with."

A voice replied—a woman's voice, unfamiliar yet

128

oddly familiar. It said, "Quickly, John. You must seize the ship."

"Who the hell . . . ?" demanded Grimes. He was at the doorway in two swift steps. He was staring at a stranger, a naked, fair-haired girl, obviously one of the women from the village. She stared at him. It was as though, he realized suddenly, somebody else were looking at him from behind her eyes.

"There is no time to lose, John. Dalzell and most of the crew are at a feast in the village. There is only a skeleton watch on board."

"Who . . . Who are you?"

The woman laughed, then replied, "Believe it or not, I'm Ken. Elena, here, is susceptible to telepathic control. She was kept on board to keep the watchkeepers company. They've been having their own party. When they passed out she collected the keys."

It made sense—or as much sense as psionic technology ever made. But it was a pity, thought Grimes, that Mayhew hadn't used this borrowed body to pick up a few hand weapons on the way down. Even so, he and the loyalists would have the advantage of surprise. Once in the control room he would have the ship's armament at his disposal; within minutes he would plaster the village with Morpheus D.

"Now you're cooking with gas!" remarked the woman approvingly in a voice that sounded more and more like Mayhew's.

"What about you and Clarisse?" asked Grimes.

"Never mind about us. Elena will release us while you're on the way to Control. But *hurry!*"

"You heard?" demanded the Commodore, turning to his cellmates. "Then come *on!*"

He brushed past the girl, ran out into the alleyway. He made his way to the axial shaft, pushed the button for the elevator. Indicator lights flashed; the cage had been only two decks below, at the Marines' messdeck. The door opened, the freed prisoners scrambled in, followed by the native woman.

"Let me—let Elena—off at the boat-bay compartment," said Mayhew through her mouth. "We're in one of the storerooms there."

"We'll wait for you there," said Grimes, pushing the right button.

"No. Get up to the control room as fast as you can. The officer of the guard woke up and is looking for Elena . . ." There was a pause. "*And* his keys. Never mind us, John. Carry on straight up."

After a second's hesitation Grimes cancelled the boat-bay compartment stop. But there was, unfortunately, no way of controlling the speed of the elevator. Its cage *was* a cage, in every sense of the word. Once the shipkeepers realized what had happened, what was happening, the prisoners would be prisoners again, trapped between decks.

The elevator jolted to a halt, just as the stridency of alarm bells shrilled throughout the ship. But luck was with Grimes and the loyalists. Whoever had cut the power had done so hastily, without checking the location of the cage. It had stopped at the level of the boat-bay compartment.

"Out!" ordered Grimes as Williams strained at the manual door control. "Out!" The floor of the cage was half a meter above deck level, but that did not matter. The compartment, now, was sealed off from the rest of the ship by the airtight doors, but that did not matter either. There was no egress either up or down, forward or aft—but there was still *out*.

Number Three was the nearer of the several

bays. "Number Three Boat!" snapped Grimes. "How is she, Bill?"

"Fine, Skipper, last time I checked. She can take us anywhere."

"Then open her up. We'll take her."

He ran behind Elena to the storeroom where Mayhew and Clarisse were confined. He snatched the bunch of magnetic keys from her hand; Ken, as he knew very well, always fumbled pitifully with even the simplest magnetic devices, and when he was controlling another's body the fumbling would be even more pronounced. He opened the door, saw Mayhew and Clarisse stretched on their benches, manacled at wrists and ankles. He released them, was briefly surprised at the agility with which they swung off their beds. But, of course, Dalzell would have allowed them to exercise under guard; he would have had uses for them.

Grimes had no need to tell the telepaths of his intentions. They followed him without question to the boat bay. As they were about to board the craft the Commodore asked suddenly, "Where's Elena?"

"She ran off as soon as I got out of her mind. She's frightened. She's hiding . . ."

"Can't you control her again? We can't leave her to face the music."

"I'm . . . I'm trying, John. But she has a strong mind. She's . . . fighting back . . ."

"What's that noise?" asked Sonya sharply.

Faintly, but audible now that the alarm bells had stopped ringing, was the wailing of a siren, an externally mounted horn. It would not be long before Dalzell and the mutineers returned from the village. And surely, thought Grimes, not even the major would blame the native girl for the escape of the prisoners. *But I wouldn't like to be in the shoes of the ship-keepers!* he told himself with grim satisfaction.

"All systems Go!" shouted Williams. "It's time we went!"

The commodore clambered into the boat, took the pilot's seat. He sealed the hull. He pressed the remote control button that should open the external door of the bay. Nothing happened; he was still looking out through the forward viewport at an unbroken sheet of metal. Whoever was in the control room had had enough sense to actuate all locking devices throughout the vessel.

But a lifeboat is a lifeboat, designed to get away from a distressed ship in practically every foreseeable combination of adverse circumstances. The emergency break-out, thought Grimes, should be working. It was. When he pushed the red button one explosive charge blew the door outwards, and another one threw the boat clear of the ship. Had the inertial drive failed to function she would have hit the village like a projectile—as it was, she blundered noisily skyward, pursued by a stream of tracer fired by somebody who was obviously not Hendriks.

"He, whoever he is," commented Williams scornfully, "would make a good gunnery officer. . . He'd make a good gunnery officer weep!"

"Don't complain," Sonya told him.

Chapter 22

The boat was spaceworthy enough and all its equipment was in good working order and it was fully stocked with emergency provisions. Grimes had no doubt of its capability to transport him and the loyalists to Mars, or to anywhere else in the Solar System. The *Quest*, with her main engines immobilized, could not pursue. Unfortunately, the ship's armament, both main and secondary, was still in working order.

Grimes turned to Mayhew. "Ken," he said urgently, "try to tune in to Hendriks. Get inside his mind, find out what he's doing, what he's going to do . . ."

"I . . . I'm already in touch. I'm picking up his thoughts. Dalzell is telling him to swat us out of the sky."

"Hell!" muttered the Commodore. And it would be hell, a brief, searing and spectacular inferno if one of *Faraway Quest's* missiles found the lifeboat. A near miss would be enough to destroy her. Her inertial drive unit was hammering flat out, but she could not hope to outrun the vicious rockets. It would be many, many minutes before she was safely out of effective range.

Grimes glanced nervously out of the viewports, saw that the others were doing the same. There was nothing to see; there would be nothing to see until the boat broke through the heavy overcast. Unless . . . Perhaps a blinding flash, and then oblivion.

Mayhew was speaking softly. "He . . . he is telling Dalzell that the self-guiding missiles are inoperable . . . But . . ." there was amazement in the telepath's voice . . . "but I think that he is lying . . ."

Grimes felt the beginning of hope. Perhaps Hendriks was not, after all, a murderer.

"*Fire* . . ." whispered Mayhew.

"Wait for it!" exclaimed Williams with spurious heartiness. "Wait for it!"

"We've no bloody option, Bill," remarked Grimes resignedly. He suppressed the temptation to throw the boat violently off course; to do so might convert a miss into a near-miss or even into a direct hit. He would stand on, trusting in whatever decency remained in the Gunnery Officer's makeup.

Then it happened.

Below and to starboard the clouds were rent apart by the explosion, by a brief and dreadful burgeoning of scarlet fire. The ambient mists vanished, flash-dried by the searing heat of the blast. The boat was driving upwards towards the domed ceiling of a roughly globular cavern of clear air in the center of which a man-made sun had been born, had lived briefly and had died. The first shock wave hit her and, even through the insulation, the doomsday crack of it was deafening. The first shock wave hit her, and then the secondary, and then the tertiary, slamming her to port and up. Grimes, sweating, fought the controls, somehow keeping the little craft steady on her heading. She was buffeted by the turbulence engendered by the detonation of the missile's warhead; it seemed that surely she must break up, spilling her people into the incandescent nothingness.

Up, Grimes pushed her. Up, up . . .

And she was clear of the overcast, although only those who had not been temporarily blinded by the blast could see the bright stars in the black sky overhead, the yellow moon, lopsided, in its last quarter, low on the eastern horizon.

Below them was the cloud—towering cumulus, vaporous peaks and pinnacles that grew and shifted and toppled, that swirled around and above the point where the rocket had burst.

"*Fire* . . ." whispered Mayhew again, echoing Hendriks' thought and spoken word.

Grimes said nothing. He knew that he must gain altitude, and yet more altitude, and even then there would be no safety. The inertial drive snarled in protest but kept going.

This time it was a salvo of three missiles, all of them well short of the target. This must have been, the Commodore realized, intentional on Hendriks' part, just as the first miss must have been intentional—although too near for comfort. The rockets burst where the boat *had* been, not where she was now. They flared dazzlingly beneath the surface of the cloud mass, turning the shadowy canyons into deep rivers of flame.

Mayhew started to laugh. It was not hysterical mirth. It was genuine amusement.

"Share the joke, Ken," snapped Sonya. "We need something to cheer us up."

"That last salvo," said the telepath, "consisted of four missiles . . ."

"I counted only three explosions," Carnaby told him.

"There were only three explosions, James. The fourth missile was a dud."

"So what?" demanded the navigator. "None of them came near us."

"That is so. But . . . But Hendriks is the gunnery specialist, and Dalzell is only a glorified infantryman. Hendriks told the Major that the first round was the ranging shot—which it most certainly was. Then, to the observers in the ship, the bursts of the second salvo, well in the clouds and practically simultaneous, looked like a single explosion. The radar showed something falling out of control and tracked it down to the sea. Hendriks knew that it was his dud missile. Dalzell thought, as he was meant to think, that it was us . . ."

"If Hendriks is so bloody loyal," growled Williams, "why isn't he here?"

"Because he doesn't want to be, Billy. He thinks he has a future on Earth . . ."

Grimes, who had been listening, chuckled. "And so he could have. After all, his given name is Thor . . ."

"Very far-fetched," commented Sonya. "And what about the others? Do none of them go down in history? Or mythology . . ."

"Those two hulking Marine privates . . ." suggested Brenda Cole. "Those twin brothers . . . Their name is Rome . . ."

"Romulus and bloody Remus? Oh, no. *No*."

"And why not, Sonya?" asked Grimes. "Come to that, the Second Engineer's name is Caine. William Caine or Bill Caine . . . Tubal Cain or Vulcan?"

His wife snorted inelegantly. "At least," she said,

"you will not realize *your* secret ambition. You will not go down in history as Zeus, father of the gods. Let us be thankful for small mercies."

The Commodore sighed. He realized wryly that his display of regret was at least half genuine. He checked the instruments, then set the controls of the boat on automatic. She would fly herself now, driving up and clear through and out of the atmosphere, until such time as course could be set. He motioned Carnaby to the seat next to his. He pointed out through the wide forward viewport to where Mars gleamed ruddily, almost a twin to the equally ruddy Antares only a few degrees to the south.

He said, "There she is, James. We've a toy computer that's little more than an electric abacus and precious little else in the way of navigational gear. We haven't even got an ephemeris. Do you think you can get us there?"

"I do, sir," replied Carnaby confidently.

"But why Mars?" demanded Sonya. "We should be safe enough from Dalzell and his mob in Earth's southern hemisphere—especially since he thinks that we've all been killed . . ."

"Hendriks *knows* that we haven't been. He's given us our chance, but he wouldn't welcome us back. Am I correct, Ken?"

"You are, John. I'll tell you what he was thinking. *And that's the last I'll see of that cantankerous old bastard! He'll not do much good for himself among the Australian aborigines . . .*"

"So Australia is definitely *out*," said Grimes. "And the Martians *may* be willing to help us."

"That'll be the sunny Friday, Skipper," said Williams. "But we'll give it a go."

"We'll give it a go," agreed Grimes.

137

Chapter 23

A lifeboat is designed to save and to sustain life; comfort is a minor consideration. Nonetheless, Grimes and his seven companions were lucky. The boat was certified to accommodate fifty persons; there were only eight people aboard it, so there was room to stretch and for the maintenance of some degree of privacy. There were six toilets—two forward, two aft and two amidships—all of them part and parcel of the boat's life support systems. In this respect the loyalists were almost as well off as they had been aboard the ship. There was a stock of the versatile, all-purpose plastic sheeting in one of the lockers, more than enough for the improvisation of separate sleeping quarters. Grimes did mutter something about "bloody gypsy tents," but nobody took him seriously. The initial supply of fresh water—which would be cycled and recycled many times before planetfall—was ample for all requirements. The food supply—mainly dehydrated concentrates—was adequate, highly nutritious and boring.

The power cells, always kept fully charged, had provided the energy needed to push the boat up clear of the atmosphere and into orbit. The initiation of the fusion reaction which was the craft's main power source took time, care and patience. The reactor's controls were so designed that anybody able to read and to follow instructions would be capable of starting the thing going, however—an absolute necessity in a vehicle which might well (as on this occasion) number no qualified engineers among its crew.

There was, of course, a powerful inertial drive unit, but neither reaction drive nor interstellar drive. But there was Carlotti equipment in addition to the Normal Space Time transceiver. The boat was incapable of making an interstellar voyage, although any Deep Space ship picking up the initial distress call (if any) from the parent vessel or from the boat itself would be able to home on the Carlotti transmitter. Voyages within a planetary system, however, were quite practicable. That from Earth to Mars, Carnaby estimated, would occupy a mere fifty days.

He told the others this while they were eating—"enjoying" would be the wrong word—their first meal in the lifeboat.

"A *mere* fifty days?" exploded Sonya. "In *this* sardine can!"

"Don't complain," Grimes told her. He went on to speak of the much longer voyages, in much worse conditions, that had been made in open boats on Earth's seas. "And at least," he concluded, "there's no danger of our having to resort to cannibalism."

"Isn't there?" demanded Sonya. She looked with

distaste at the pallid mess in the bowl of her spoon. "Isn't there? After a few weeks of this . . . *goo* we might feel like it!"

"Cheer up, Sonya," Williams admonished her. "The first fifty years are the worst!"

"I said 'days,' not 'years,' Commander," corrected Carnaby.

"Fifty days . . ." said Grimes thoughtfully. "Ample time to get ourselves organized—but not too much time. To begin with we must try to get it through to the Martians that we come in peace. That's your department, Ken and Clarisse. Try to get in touch with that local telepath again. Play the poor, helpless castaway angle for all you're worth!"

"And poor, helpless castaways is just what we are," commented Sonya.

"Mphm. Not so helpless, as long as we have a ship of sorts under us. But there's no point in telling the Martians that. Now, has anybody else any suggestions?" He added, looking at his wife, "Constructive ones, that is."

"I was rather wondering, sir," asked Ruth Macoboy diffidently, "if I should try to get in touch too. Our NST transceiver, on a tight beam, has a very long range . . ."

Grimes considered this. He said at last, "We're up against the language barrier, Ruth. Ken and Clarisse, working with ideas rather than words, aren't . . . Mphm. But a beamed signal, even if it's no more than a repetition of a Morse symbol, will tell them that we're coming, that we aren't trying to slink up on them, as it were . . ."

"Assuming that *they* are tuned in and listening," said Sonya.

"They probably will be," said Grimes, "once the telepathic contact has been established." He thought, *It doesn't matter, anyhow. The main con-*

sideration is keeping as many people as possible fully employed on a voyage like this. In some ways—in one way—Bligh was lucky. During his boat voyage after the Bounty mutiny he charted everything along his track.

"Can't anything be done about the food?" asked Sonya.

Grimes turned to Brenda Coles. "That's your department, Brenda. What has *Faraway Quest's* Assistant Bio-Chemist to suggest?" He grinned. "My apologies. As far as this boat is concerned, you're *the* Bio-Chemist."

The small, plump blonde smiled back at him. "This *is* rather grim, isn't it? But I hope that the next meal will be better. There's a supply of flavoring essences in the galley—chicken, steak, lobster, and coffee, chocolate, vanilla . . . The trouble is that I've never been much of a cook . . ."

"*Your* department, then, Sonya," said Grimes. "Ruth will measure out for each meal what we need in the way of proteins, vitamins and whatever to keep us functioning. You will try to turn these basic requirements into something palatable."

"Chicken mole . . ." murmured Sonya thoughtfully.

"And what's that?" demanded Williams. "I've heard rabbit referred to as underground chicken . . ."

"Really, Bill," she said reprovingly. "Chicken mole is a Mexican dish. Chicken with mole sauce. The mole sauce is made mainly from bitter chocolate."

"Gah!" exclaimed Williams.

"And the other main ingredient of the sauce," Grimes told him, "is dried chicken blood. Mphm. I don't think, somehow, that we shall be having chicken mole on the menu. Anyhow, do your best, ladies. And remember that there's no risk of the customers deciding to patronize another restaurant..."

"There's always the risk of their murdering the chef!" said Williams cheerfully.

But it wouldn't come to that, Grimes hoped. His people would be keeping themselves occupied during the seven long weeks of the voyage. Williams there was no need to worry about—*he* would always find something useful to do. And as long as Carnaby could navigate, *he* would be happy. And if time did hang heavily, in spite of everything, there was the games locker, with chess, Scrabble and the like, as well as packs of playing cards and sets of dice. This would be no luxury cruise, but it could have been a lot worse.

Chapter 24

It was a long, long drag from Earth to Mars.

They had made much longer voyages, all of them, but in conditions which, compared to those in the lifeboat, were fantastically luxurious. There had been organized entertainment and ample facilities for self-entertainment. There had been a well-varied menu and meals had been occasions to look forward to. In the boat meals were something to be gotten through as expeditiously as possible. In spite of the skill of Sonya and Brenda, in spite of the wide variety of flavorings, the goo was still goo. Texture is as important as taste and appearance.

Of them all, Carnaby was the happiest. Grimes almost regretted that the navigator had been one of the officers remaining loyal to him. He, the Commodore, had always loved navigation, had always maintained that it was an art rather than a science. But he had always maintained, too, that it is rather pointless to keep a dog and to bark oneself. So . . . So Carnaby was the navigating officer. Carnaby was a direct descendant of those navigators who, in the days of sail on Earth's seas, had been called "artists." Grimes helped Carnaby when he was asked to, but this was not very often.

Out from Earth's orbit, in a widely arcing trajectory, swept the boat, its inertial drive unit hammering away with never a missed beat. Through the interplanetary emptiness—the near-emptiness—it flew, with the ruddy spark that was Mars at first wide on the bow but, with every passing day, the bearing closing. Carnaby was shooting at a moving target and, ideally, his missile (of which he was part) would arrive at Point X at precisely the same second as its objective. From a mere spark the red planet expanded to an appreciable disc, even to the naked eye. Astern, on the quarter, the blazing sun diminished appreciably.

Meanwhile Ken and Clarisse Mayhew rarely stirred from the little tent of plastic sheeting that they had made their private quarters—but they were not idle. Now and again Grimes would hear their soft voices as they vocalized their thoughts, their psionic transmissions. *Castaways calling Mars . . . Castaways calling Mars . . . Do you hear me? Come in please. Come in . . . Come in . . .* The radio-telephonic jargon sounded strange in these circumstances, but its use was logical enough.

On they drove, on, and on.

Mars was a globe now, an orange beach ball floating in the black sea of Space, its surface darkly mottled, the polar frost cap gleaming whitely. It was time, Carnaby announced, for deceleration. He and Grimes took their places at the controls, turned the lifeboat about its short axis until the thrust of the drive was pushing them away from the planetary objective instead of towards it. It would be days, however, before the braking effect was fully felt.

And then Mayhew came out from his tent and said, "John, I have them. I have the same man that I had before, when they gave us the bum's rush . . ."

Grimes made the last adjustment to his set of controls, said to Carnaby, "She's all yours, James." Then, to Mayhew, "Any joy, Ken?"

"I . . . I think so, John. They aren't overjoyed to learn that we're on our way to them, but they realize, I think, that we have no place else to go. We can land, they say, as long as we don't get underfoot."

"Decent of them. No, I'm not being sarcastic. After the exhibition that Hendriks put on the last time that we were out this way it's not surprising that they don't want to know us. Mphm. Well, I suggest that you go into a huddle with Ruth—frequencies and all that—and try to get them to set up some sort of radio beacon for us to home on. We'll set this little bitch down exactly where they want us to . . ."

"Into the jaws of a trap, perhaps," suggested Sonya pesimistically.

"No, Sonya. They aren't that sort of people," Mayhew told her.

"I sincerely hope that you're right."

"I am right," he said shortly. "In fact, now that they have learned quite a lot about us, they are hinting that they may be able to help us. After all, their level of technology is a high one."

"From you," she said, "that *is* praise."

"Machines have their uses," he admitted.

And Grimes thought, *Can they get us back to where and when we belong? Science or black magic—what does it matter as long as it gets the right results . . .*

Chapter 25

Slowly the boat dropped down through the clear Martian sky, its inertial drive muttering irritably, riding the beam of the radio beacon that had been set up on the bank of one of the minor canals. The line of approach took them well clear of any city, although a sizeable metropolis could just be seen, a cluster of fragile towers on the far northern horizon. There were no villages within view, no small towns. There was only the desert, ochre under the bright sunlight, with a broad, straight band of irrigation sweeping across it from north to south, a wide, dark green ribbon down the center of which ran a gleaming line of water.

In some ways this Mars was not unlike the terraformed Mars that Grimes had known (would know). The air was a little thinner, perhaps, and there was less water—but it was, even so, utterly dissimilar to the almost dead world upon which the first explorers from Earth had made their landing. Nonetheless, this was a dying world. There was an autumnal quality in the light, bright though it was

. . . *Rubbish*! he told himself angrily. But the feeling persisted.

The commodore had the controls, and Carnaby was visibly sulking. Grimes was more amused than otherwise by his navigator's reaction to his taking charge at the finish. Meanwhile, he watched the needle of the improvised radio compass, keeping the boat exactly on course. Carnaby had done well, he thought, very well—but he, Grimes, was entitled to his fun now and again. Carnaby had done well, and so had all of the others. Clarisse and Ken Mayhew were mathematical morons, but the minds of Carnaby and Ruth Macoboy had been opened to them, and the telepaths, working with their opposite numbers on Mars, had been able to cope with with the task of setting up a radio-navigational system. Fortunately mathematics is a universal language, and the basic laws of physics are valid anywhere in the known Galaxy . . .

"There's a light!" called Carnaby, who was in the co-pilot's seat, pointing.

Yes, there was a light, winking, brilliantly scarlet against the dark green. The commodore switched his attention from the radio compass to the visual mark. With his free hand he picked up the binoculars, studied the landing place. There were buildings there, he saw, although they seemed to be little more than plastic igloos. But there was no sign of an airstrip or a landing apron. This did not much matter, as the boat would be set down vertically— but Grimes was reluctant to crush what looked like a crop of food plants during his landing.

"It's all right, John," said Mayhew. "They aren't worried about this last harvest. They will not be needing it."

"Mphm?" But if Mayhew said so, then this was the way it was.

147

Grimes reduced speed as he lost altitude, coming in at little more than a crawl. The downthrust of the drive produced a wake of crushed vegetation. This effect could have been avoided by coming in over the canal itself—but it was too late to think about that now. In any case, he had Mayhew's word for it that it didn't matter. Finally he dropped the boat to the ground no more than a meter from the flashing beacon. He looked out through the ports at the cluster of plastic domes. What now?

A circular doorway appeared in the skin of the nearer one. A figure appeared in the opening. It was not unmanlike, but was unhumanly thin and tall, and the shape of the head was cylindrical rather than roughly spherical. But it had two arms, two legs, two eyes and a mouth.

"Dwynnaith," said Mayhew. "He is here to meet us..."

"Where's the red carpet?" demanded Williams.

Mayhew ignored this. "His people may be able to help us. But, first, he wishes to inspect the boat."

"Tell him," said Grimes, "that this is Liberty Hall, that he can..."

"I'm rather tired of that expression," interrupted Sonya.

"Just convey the correct impression, then," Grimes said. "And tell him that we're sorry not to be able to receive him on board with the proper hospitality."

"That," Mayhew assured the commodore, "is the very least of their worries. At this particular point of their history they regard us as a nuisance. Luckily, some of their mathematicians are intrigued by our predicament and have decided to help us." He smiled slightly. "By helping us they are also getting us out of their hair."

Grimes pushed the buttons that would open the door and extrude the ramp. He remarked, as he did so, "I was brought up never to look a gift horse in the mouth. As long as they help us I shall be grateful, and not worry about their motivation."

Dwynnaith clambered into the boat. He was all arms and legs, and his garments of metal and plastic gleamed like the chitinous integument of an insect. He exuded a vaguely unpleasant dry, musty odor. He creaked as he moved. He ignored Grimes, Williams, Carnaby, Sonya, Ruth Macoboy and Brenda Coles, went straight to Mayhew and Clarisse. He extended a three-fingered hand on the end of a spidery arm, touched first Mayhew and then Clarisse lightly on the forehead. They responded, although they had to reach up to return the salutation.

Escorted by the human telepaths, he made his slow way aft until he came to the boat's Carlotti transceiver. He stared at the instrument with his huge lidless eyes for at least a minute, then touched the antenna with his left hand. The elliptical Mobius Strip rotated slowly about its long axis in response to the impulse of his thin finger. He looked at it, standing in motionless silence, for about five minutes. It was impossible to read any expression on that almost featureless face.

"Well?" asked Grimes at last. "Well?"

"I—we—think that it is well, John," said Mayhew. "He is reporting what he is observing to his colleagues in the city. They, in turn, are passing the information on to the mathematicians . . ."

But what the hell, Grimes asked himself, *has our Carlotti transceiver to do with their helping us?* Then he remembered—or did the picture come from outside his mind?—the towers of the city they had seen, each of which had what looked like a Carlotti antenna at its highest point.

Mayhew spoke again. "We are to stay here, John, until sent for. We can live aboard the boat or in the temporary dwellings, as we please. Meanwhile *they* would like to take our Carlotti set to the city to study it and—as far as I can gather—make the necessary modifications. If Ruth will unbolt it from the bulkhead . . ."

"Modifications?" demanded Grimes. "What modifications? And what for?"

"I'm no wiser than you are, John. All that I know is that it's somehow important. They must have it if they're to help us. They haven't the time to produce a similar, suitably miniaturized instrument of their own."

"Do as the man says, Ruth," ordered Grimes. "Or do as the Martian says."

As Mayhew and Clarisse escorted Dwynnaith from the boat she had assembled her tools ready to start work.

Chapter 26

Dwynnaith returned to the city in a blimp-like airship that came out for him. Carnaby, watching the clumsy-seeming contraption approaching, said, "A gasbag? A dirigible balloon? I thought these people were highly advanced, but . . ."

"And what's wrong with it, James?" Grimes asked him. "Why consume power just to stay aloft when, with aerostatic lift, you do it for free?"

"But the speed of the thing . . . Or the lack of speed, rather . . ."

"If you're in no great hurry," said the commodore, "an airship is at least as good as any other form of transport."

The Martian, still silent, was obviously communing with Mayhew. Then the telepath said, "He wants us to keep well away from the beacon, John."

"Why, Ken?"

"I'm . . . I'm not quite sure. Some mechanical technicality about anchoring . . ."

It was a pity, thought Grimes, that Mayhew was such a moron in all matters concerning machinery. But, probably, the airship would be lowering some kind of grapnel. It made sense. He and the others moved well away from the immediate vicinity of the still-flashing beacon.

The airship was by no means as primitive as it had seemed from a distance. As it approached it lost altitude, and Grimes could see the silvery mesh that enclosed the ballonnettes tightening, compressing the gasbags, reducing buoyancy. Here was no wasteful valving of gas. The ship came in very slowly at the finish, its single, pusher airscrew just ticking over. When it was almost directly over the beacon it stopped. There was a loud *thung!* and a metal projectile shot out and down from the gondola, burying itself in the soil. As it did so the grapnel arms opened, to grip firmly. The mooring line—a flexible wire, pencil-thin—tightened as a winch in the airship took the strain, hauling it down for the last few meters. Then it floated there, riding quietly to the slight breeze, the skids of its undercarriage just clear of the tops of the green plants.

Dwynnaith stood a little apart from the humans, issuing what sounded like a rapid-fire stream of orders. So he *could* speak, and so the airship's crew were not telepaths, thought Grimes. His voice was painfully shrill, as were the voices that answered him from inside the gondola. It was like the chirping of insects, or of birds. *Like birds?* wondered the commodore, the beginning of a wild surmise taking vague shape in his mind. Like birds? Somehow that tied in with the autumnal feel in the air. There was some correlation—but what?

Dwynnaith clambered with atthtopoidal agility up a short ladder that was extended from the open door of the gondola. Grimes noted that as his weight came on it the gasbag was allowed to expand in compensation. He stood in the doorway which, although narrow, was quite wide enough to accommodate both himself and one of the crew members. The two attenuated beings were obviously waiting for something.

"The Carlotti transceiver . . ." said Mayhew.

The dismantled instrument was handed up and taken inside. The door slid shut. Abruptly the anchor jerked from the ground, its blades retracting. The airship bounded upwards, turning in a wide arc as it did so, flew steadily northwards. Soon it was no more than an almost invisible dot in the clear sky.

"And what happens now?" asked Carnaby.

"We wait," said Mayhew.

"For what?" demanded Sonya.

"If I knew, I'd tell you," replied the telepath testily.

So they waited.

They decided to live in the plastic domes that had been set up for their use; the temporary, inflatable dwellings offered far more comfort and privacy than the cramped quarters of the lifeboat. The furniture—beds and chairs and tables of a sort, also inflatable—must have been especially made with human proportions in mind. There was no heating, although this did not much matter as the double skin formed adequate insulation against the coldness of the Martian night, and there was a good supply of blankets woven from some synthetic fibre. There was no lighting, but portable lamps could be brought in from the boat. There were no cooking facilities, but the lifeboat's galley could be used for the preparation of meals. No food was provided, but the boat's stores were very far from being exhausted.

There was food growing all around them, of course. The boat carried the means whereby spacemen stranded on an alien planet could test local foodstuffs to determine their suitability or otherwise for human consumption, and Brenda Coles was a qualified biochemist. She announced that the bean-like crop among which they were sitting was not only edible; it was highly nutritious. Unfortunately the flavor was vile, and nothing could be done to kill the taste.

Grimes said, after an experimental nibble and hasty spitting out, "Perhaps we *would* have been better off in Australia . . . Even witchety grubs'd taste better than this!"

He was not, after the first day or so, happy. There was so little to do. He would have liked to have taken the boat to make a detailed exploration of the countryside—but this, Mayhew assured him, would most certainly not be approved by the Martians. "We must stay here, John," he said firmly. "We must be ready to go to the city as soon as they send for us. Bear in mind that we are uninvited guests and that we must do nothing, nothing at all, to antagonize our hosts."

"But they *will* help us?"

"They think that they will be able to help us."

And with that Grimes had to be satisfied.

Of them all, only Brenda Coles seemed to be reasonably content. She was only a biochemist, not a xenobiologist, but she possessed a smattering of xenobiology and occupied herself by attempting to catalogue the flora and fauna in the vicinity of the camp. Carnaby helped her, although not with over-much enthusiasm. He complained, out of her hearing, "Damn it all, I'm a navigator, not a butter-fly hunter!"

Not that the butterflies, so-called, *were* butterflies. They were winged arthropods of a sort—but arthropods are not warm-blooded, and these things were. In spite of this they had not survived the millennia prior to Man's first landing on Mars—but neither had much of anything else, plant or animal. Perhaps the great meteor shower which formed the craters had wiped out practically all life on the Red Planet—or would wipe out all life.

"But what about the cities?" asked Grimes, when this theory was advanced. "You can't tell me that each meteor had the name of a city written on it. There must have been *something* left for Men to find."

"But there wasn't," said Williams.

"No. There wasn't—save for a couple or three dubious artifacts."

"I think . . ." began Mayhew hesitantly, "I think that we arrived just before some sort of mass migration . . . An old world, senescent, and its people moving on to greener, fresher pastures . . ."

Carnaby picked up the home-made butterfly net that he had been using, pretended to strum it as though it were a guitar.

"I've laid around and played around, this old town too long," he sang.

"Summer almost gone, winter comin' on . . .

"I've laid around and played around this old town too long,

"An' I feel I gotta travel on . . ."

"Mphm," grunted Grimes. "Yes, there is that sort of feel in the air. But . . ." Then he, too, sáng, in spite of Sonya's protests.

"There's a lonesome train at six oh eight a-comin' through the town,

"*A-comin' through the town, an' I'll be home-ward bound,*

"*There's a lonesome train at six oh eight a-comin' through the town . . .*

"*An' I feel I gotta travel on . . .*"

"No one's stopping you," said his wife acidly.

"You don't get the point. When you board that lonesome train you don't take the town with you. You leave it behind. You leave town, in fact."

"What are you drivin' at, Skipper?" asked Williams.

"I . . . I don't quite know. When I was a kid, when I was a cadet at the Survey Service academy, we were supposed to read selected Twentieth Century science fiction. Wild stuff, most of it, and well off the beam most of the time. And yet, after years, some of it sticks in my memory. There was one story about an invention called, I think, the spindizzy. It was a sort of anti-gravitational device that lifted entire cities and sent them whiffling around the galaxy as enormous spaceships with closed economies . . .

"What if the Martians have something of the kind in mind? What if those antennae on the towers of their cities, like Carlotti antennae, aren't for communication but are something on the same general lines as our Mannschenn Drive? After all, both the Mannschenn Drive and the Carlotti Communication System do funny things to Space and Time . . . Mphm. It could be that they've taken our Carlotti set so they can modify it so it can be used as an interstellar drive for the boat . . ."

"And if they have, if they can," asked Sonya, "where do we go to? And, come to that, why?"

Carnaby started to sing again.

"*Sheriff an' police a-comin' after me,*

"*Comin' after me, a-comin' after me . . .*

156

THE WAY BACK

"Sheriff an' police a-comin' after me,
"An' I feel I gotta travel on . . ."

Nobody thought that it was very funny.

Chapter 27

The summons came an hour before sunrise.

Mayhew woke Grimes and Sonya, while Clarisse called the others.

Grimes asked, struggling into his clothes, "So this is it?"

"This is it, John."

"What is this *it*?" demanded Sonya grumpily.

"I . . . I don't know. *They* seem determined not to let me have a detailed picture. But you must be able to *feel* it . . . An atmosphere of tense expectancy . . . The bustle of embarkation . . ."

Sonya sniffed audibly, then said, "Fort Sumter has been fired upon. My regiment marches at dawn."

"I don't get it . . ." said Mayhew, after a puzzled pause.

"I do," Grimes told him. "But get into the boat, Ken. And we'll leave none of our own gear behind. Come to that, we may as well take these blankets. They might come in useful . . ."

158

Grimes and Sonya, muffled against the cold, emerged from the dome into the pre-dawn darkness. There was a thin, chill wind, and overhead the sky was clear, the stars bitterly bright. To the east the horizon was black against the first pale flush of day and a bright planet blazed with a greenish effulgence. Earth . . . And what were the mutineers doing, wondered the commodore. And what was happening, what would happen, to his ship, to the old *Quest*? Grimes looked away from the distant home world to the west, where tiny Phobos was slowly rising. Deimos, even tinier, was among the stars somewhere, undistinguishable from them. He had no time to waste determining its exact location. And to the north was the glare of the city lights.

Lights were coming on in the lifeboat. The loud grumbling of the inertial drive unit shattered the early morning calm. Williams must be already aboard, ensuring that all was in a state of readiness.

Grimes and Sonya hurried to the boat, clambered in through the open door. Yes, Williams was there, in the co-pilot's seat, and Clarisse, Mayhew, Carnaby, Brenda and Ruth were in their places.

"All right," said the commodore. "Let's go." He eased himself into his chair. "To the city, I suppose, Ken?"

"To the city. We are to land in the central plaza."

The hammering of the inertial drive became louder as Grimes lifted the boat. She lurched, steadied. Below her the canal was a ribbon of faintly gleaming silver in the starlight. Ahead the city was a star cluster on the black horizon, individual lights now visible through the dim-glowing haze.

As they flew on, the rosy pallor in the east

159

spread slowly over the entire sky and the ochreous desert reflected the growing luminosity. Abruptly, a point of dazzling light appeared over the low hills, expanded rapidly. The sun was up, and the towers of the city stood stark and black in the pearly morning mist, but only for an instant; the clarity of their first appearance dimmed to a quivering insubstantiality. Grimes remembered again that story which he had read so long ago; what was its title? *Cities in Flight?* Something like that. He laughed briefly. *Just a trick of the light,* he told himself.

They flew on—and, quite suddenly, were rattling over the pinnacles of the outermost towers. On each of them gleamed the elliptical Mobius strip, but the antennae were motionless. Over broad avenues they flew, slowly now, over the graceful bridges that spanned the wide streets, that connected tower to tower in a complex mesh. There was traffic abroad—beetle-like vehicles, small knots of pedestrians, most of whom paused briefly to look upwards at the noisy flying boat.

They came to the central plaza, which was circular in plan, paved with lustrous pink stone, and ornamented by a central fountain and a profusion of flowering shrubs. To the north of the fountain a space had been cleared for them—shrubs removed, their beds flattened. So that there could be no mistake, a little red-flashing beacon indicated their landing site.

"I suppose this is where they want us," said Grimes.

"It is," Mayhew told him.

"Mphm. I think I can wriggle us in without knocking anything over," said Grimes.

Cautiously he brought the boat down. There was just room for her between the beds of shrubs and

160

the stone benches. When her landing gear crunched on the paving he cut the drive. He said, unnecessarily, "Well, we're here."

Sonya muttered something about a blinding glimpse of the obvious but she, with the others, was staring out through the viewports. From ground level the towers were even more impressive than they had appeared from the air. They soared like fountains, flash-frozen to immobility. They, and the connecting bridges, were an arching spray of intricately interlacing stone and metal. Over all, glittering gold in the sunlight, were those enigmatic antennae.

"Company," announced Williams prosaically.

Grimes pulled his regard away from the fantastic architecture, looked to where the commander was pointing. Walking slowly towards the boat came a small procession, six Martians, all of them tall, attenuated, all with those almost featureless elongated heads, all of them looking more like insects than men. Two of them carried between them the Carlotti transceiver. It looked just as it had when it had been dismantled, but it was impossible to see what changes had been made to the components concealed by the casing.

"Dwynnaith is with them," said Mayhew. His lips went on moving, silently, as he put his thoughts into words. Then, "We are to accompany him to the assembly hall. The others will fit the . . . the apparatus back into the boat."

"Very well," said Grimes at last. He did not like the idea of letting strangers, aliens, loose in the lifeboat without himself or one of his people there to see what was being done, but realized that he had no option. "Very well."

Mayhew and Clarisse were first out of the boat. They went through the head-touching ceremony with Dwynnaith. The other Martians looked at the humans with an apparent lack of curiosity, conversed among themselves in eerie, chittering voices. Grimes was last on the ground. He waited until the telepaths seemed to have completed their silent conversation, then said, "We're all ready, Ken."

"Good. The Council is waiting for us."

The Council was waiting for them in a great hall on the ground floor of one of the towers. It was a huge room, with a vast expanse of polished floor, a high, vaulted ceiling, a platform against one wall. There was neither ornamentation nor furniture, save for the eight inflatable chairs for the humans, incongruous in the vastness. Six of these chairs were on the floor before the platform, the other two were on the platform itself.

On the dais stood the members of the Council—ten of them, all tall, all attenuated, each one indistiguishable, to human eyes, from any of the others. Dwynnaith joined them on the platform, accompanied by Mayhew and Clarisse. He stood behind their chairs as they seated themselves.

"Is it all right for us to sit?" asked Grimes.

"That is what the chairs are for, John," replied Mayhew.

The humans seated themselves. They looked up at the grave Martians, the Martians looked down at them. The silence was becoming oppressive. Grimes wished that he had his pipe with him—and that he had something with which to fill it.

Mayhew spoke again—but it was not, somehow, his voice. Just as he had controlled the girl Elena, Grimes realized, somebody or something was now controlling him. His face was the face of a humanoid robot, mobile yet not really alive.

He said, "I, Gwayllian, Moderator of the

Council, have studied and learned your language. It is not possible for my vocal chords to form the necessary sounds, therefore I speak through the mouth of Mayhew. You will forgive me if my vocabulary is in any way deficient."

"You're doin' fine," remarked the irrepressible Williams.

"I thank you. But you will please not interrupt. The time fast approaches when we, when we all, must . . . go. But before our departure you should know what is about to happen.

"The first time that you came to this world, which you call Mars, we wanted nothing of you. Your landing, in your ship, would have interfered with our preparations for the . . . voyage. You were, with all the resources of your own technology at your disposal, quite capable of . . . looking after yourselves. The second time that you came, as fugitives, our preparations were almost complete. You were in no way a menace to our plans. Our engineers, our mathematicians, our scientists could spare the time to consider your problem. The solution of it was an amusing mental exercise.

"But, as a beginning, I must tell you who and what we are.

"We are not of this world. Many millennia ago our people lived on another planet, many light years from here. The name of the sun, the star, around which it revolved would be meaningless to you; besides, that star is no more. We—our ancestors—escaped before our sun became a nova. Our ships dispersed. One ship found this planet which, as it was then, was almost a twin to the one which we had abandoned. Slowly, over the centuries, we rebuilt our civilization. But slowly, over the long centuries, this world was dying. Rejuvenation of the planet was considered; this would have been a

far from impossible feat. But our astronomers
warned of an inevitable, coming catastrophe. An
extrapolation of the orbits of Mars, as you call this
world, and of sundry planetoids made it obvious
that a disastrous meteoric bombardment could not
be avoided.

"Yet we did not wish to leave this planet, even
though we still possessed the technology for fast-
er-than-light travel between the stars. It had become home. We did not wish to leave our cities,
which had grown up with us. But there was a way.
There was a way to avoid the inevitable wreck, to
save our cities as well as ourselves. And we took
it."

He's getting his tenses mixed, thought Grimes.
He said—some comment seemed to be expected—
"So you will convert your cities into FTL
spaceships . . ."

"Not *will*," replied Mayhew in that voice which
was not his own. "Not *will*, but *did*. And not space
ships, but time ships. We went back in Time to a
period just prior to the landing of our ancestors, so
that they found the civilization which they, themselves, had founded already well established and
flourishing. We have repeated the cycle now a
thousand times, on each occasion with only minor
variations.

"You will be such a variation—and a very minor
one."

Somewhere a great bell was tolling, slow,
measured strokes.

A countdown, thought Grimes, *a temporal
countdown* . . . He said desperately, "Suppose that
we don't want to come with you?"

"You and your people may stay if you wish.
You may hope to survive the meteoric storm which

will wreck this world, or you may return to Earth. But do not forget that we offer you hope."

"Give it a go, Skipper," urged Williams. "Give it a go. What have we to lose?"

"Nothing," said the Moderator of the Council through Mayhew. "Nothing, but there may be— there just may be—much to gain. And now you will return to your boat."

Chapter 28

They hurried back to the boat.

It lay there, in the center of the plaza, glistening in the fine spray that was blowing over it from the fountain. The Martian technicians had finished their work and were gone. The Carlotti transceiver was back in its old place. It was Sonya who noticed that the blankets they had brought from the encampment had gone. It seemed a matter of no great importance—but, thought Grimes, it looked as though it had been decided that they were to take no local artifacts with them to wherever—or whenever—they were being sent.

"Button up, Skipper?" asked Williams.

"Yes, we'd better," Grimes told him.

The doors slid shut, sealing the hull.

What was going to happen now? That great bell was still tolling with slow, solemn deliberation, measuring off the remaining minutes of time. The plaza was deserted, as were the streets and the bridges. There was a brooding atmosphere of tense expectancy.

Grimes said, more to himself than to anybody else, "I wonder if we're supposed to switch on the Carlotti . . ." He walked slowly to the instrument, put out his finger to the On-Off button. But it was no longer there. The panel was featureless. "Ruth!" he called. "Come here! What do you make of this?"

Then the bell stopped, and the silence was like a heavy blow. "Look!" shouted Carnaby. "Look!"

They looked. Atop the towers surrounding the plaza the antennae were starting to rotate, slowly at first, about their long axes, the sunlight flashing from the polished, twisted surfaces. And—"Look!" cried Ruth Macoboy. The miniature antenna of the Carlotti transceiver was rotating too, in synchronization. Slowly at first, then faster and faster, the sun was setting, falling back towards the eastern horizon. Abruptly there was deep shadow as it was obscured by the towers. Then there was twilight, but morning not evening twilight, come again. There was twilight, and night, and day, with the sun rising in the west and setting in the east.

Night followed day and day followed night, faster and faster, a flicker of alternating light and darkness that became too fast to register on the retina, that was seen as a grey dusk. Overhead the sun was a wavering band of yellow light in the sky, with Phobos as a narrower, dimmer band. The stars were streaks of silver.

Yet the buildings surrounding the plaza were still substantial, were glowing with a hard luminosity. The whirling antennae at their pinnacles flared like torches in the dimness.

For hours this went on.

It was fascinating to watch, at first, but the fascination wore off. One can get used to anything in time. Brenda Coles left the port beside which she was seated, went into the little galley. She returned with mugs of instant coffee, which all of them sipped gratefully. It was not very good coffee, but the very ordinariness of what they were doing was psychologically beneficial. They talked a little, in disjointed sentences. They wondered what was going to happen next, more for the sake of idle speculation than in the hope that any questions would be answered thereby.

Said Grimes, "I hope that we are able to watch the first colonists landing. I'd like to see what sort of ship they have . . ."

Williams said, "It must be about time for our learned friends to start putting on the brakes . . . I don't know *when* we are—but at this rate we shall be slung back to the birth of the Solar System . . ."

"Our Carlotti antenna is still spinning as fast as ever," commented Ruth Macoboy. "They must have fitted it with new bearings . . ."

"Mphm?" grunted Grimes. He looked into his empty mug. "Any more of this vile brew, Brenda?"

"I'll get some for you, Commodore."

"Don't bother. A short stroll to the galley will stretch my legs."

He got to his feet. He glanced out through the nearest viewport. The mug dropped from his hand, bounced noisily on the deck.

"What's wrong?" asked Sonya sharply.

"Something," he said at last. "Something is very much wrong!"

He thought bitterly, *The bastards! They said all along that they didn't want us, and now they've got rid of us!*

No longer were the towers of the city visible from the viewports. Outside was just a featureless

168

landscape, although overhead the sun and the larger moon still were arches of light in the grey sky. The boat was still falling through Time, but the city must have been left many years in the future. And that city, Grimes realized, had been to the boat no more than a temporal booster, analagous to the first stage of a primitive space rocket, a booster that had given the small craft escape velocity from Now.

"Ruth," he said, "stop that bloody thing!"

"I . . . I can't, Commodore. There are no controls . . ."

"Open it up. Take a hammer to it. An axe . . ."

"No," said Mayhew. "*No.*"

"And why not?"

"Can't you see, John? This is intentional . . ."

"I know bloody well it's intentional. Your longheaded friends put over a far better marooning stunt than even Dalzell could have managed. We must stop this blasted time machine before it's too late, and then we return to Earth . . ."

"And get nibbled by dinosaurs, John?" asked Sonya. "No, thank you. Hear Ken out before you do anything rash."

"We must have faith . . ." persisted the telepath.

"Faith?"

"They meant us no harm, John. They were doing their best for us. They gave us a chance to get back to our own Time . . ."

"Looks like it, doesn't it?"

Grimes glared through the port. Was that water out there, a vast, sullen sea? How far back had they come? Seas on Mars? Was that water, or was it barren rock, glowing incandescently, flowing like water? Was it molten rock—or a fire mist?

Was it a fire mist—or nothingness?

The nothingness before the birth of the worlds, of the suns, of the universe itself . . .

There is no place to go, thought Grimes.

"There is no place to go," he said.

"But there will be," stated Mayhew with an odd certainty. "There will be, or there was. There must be."

"I'll make some more coffee," said Brenda Coles.

Chapter 29

Time, subjective time, passed.

The boat hung in a formless nothingness, an empty void. And yet, Grimes knew, she was not in a vacuum. She was afloat in a vast sea of hydrogen atoms, the building blocks of the universe. She was afloat, and she was adrift. To have started the inertial drive would have been pointless; there was no place to go. Furthermore nobody, not even Carnaby, was mathematician enough to work out the possible consequences. The antenna of the modified Carlotti transceiver was still whirring about its long axis, and who could say what the resultant would be if motion in Space were added to the motion in Time?

She hung there, motionless, a tiny bubble of light and life in the all-pervading nothingness. She hung there, while her crew went about the dreary business of staying alive apathetically, gulping at regular intervals their unappetizing meals, maintaining, without enthusiasm, the machinery that ensured their continued survival. Brenda Coles was beginning to look worried, however. Their stores, although ample to begin with, would not last forever. She reported the dangerous depletion of foodstuffs to Grimes.

He said, "We shall have to ration ourselves."

"Luckily," remarked Sonya, "that is no great hardship."

"Not with this tucker," agreed Williams.

"I think," said Carnaby hesitantly, "that we may be getting somewhere at last. Or somewhen . . ."

"Masterly navigation, James," said Williams. "If you can find your way through this interstellar fog you're a super genius!"

Carnaby took offense. "Nobody could find his way in *this*, Commander, and you know it. But it seems to me that there's the start of a definite luminosity . . ."

"The heat death of the Universe in reverse . . ." murmured Grimes. "The wheel always comes full circle, no matter which way it's spinning . . ."

"James is right," stated Brenda Coles firmly. "It *is* getting lighter."

There was an intense, dreadful flare of radiation, dazzling, blinding, but lasting for only an infinitesimal fraction of a second. When at last Grimes was able to reopen his watering, smarting eyes, he thought that what he was seeing was only a persistent after image, a wavering band of dull crimson light that bisected the blackness outside the viewport. But it did not fade; it seemed, instead, to be growing steadily brighter.

"The sun . . ." he whispered.

"The sun . . ." murmured Williams. "This is where we came in."

"No. Not yet. But we have to think about stopping that infernal contraption the Martians planted on us. Not yet, but as soon as conditions outside seem capable of supporting life . . ."

"Still desert, by the looks of it," Williams said. "Sand. Nothing but sand . . ."

Sand, nothing but sand, and then a hint of green under the blue-grey sky, the yellow sun. Sand, and the green area spreading . . . The greenness spreading, flickering through its seasonal changes, but spreading . . . And was that a cluster of white buildings? They appeared briefly, and were gone, but there were others, larger ones where they had stood, their outlines firmer, more solid.

Again there was the flickering that they had experienced at the start of this voyage, the rapid alternation of light and dark as day followed night, as day followed night, the periods growing longer, hours passing in seconds and then in minutes . . .

The antenna of the Carlotti transceiver was rotating more slowly now, its shape could clearly be seen. It was slowing down, slowing down, and the rate of temporal regression was slowing with it. It was slowing down, spinning lazily, stopping . . .

There was a muffled explosion. Acrid smoke billowed from the cabinet.

But Grimes hardly noticed. He was staring out of the port at a familiar sight. The boat was resting on a concrete apron, clean and bright under the noon sun. Along the perimeter were spaceport administration buildings; from a flagstaff atop the control tower flew the blue, star-spangled flag of the Interstellar Federation. And there were ships— one of the Federation's Constellation Class cruisers, a couple of Serpent Class couriers.

"Where are we?" Carnaby was asking. "Where are we?"

"Still on Mars," Grimes told him. "The neatly terraformed Mars that I used to know when I was in the Survey Service. Marsport, the Survey Service Base . . ." He started to cough as the smoke from the explosion reached him. "Open her up, Bill. The air's quite good. It was when I was here last, anyhow."

He stayed aboard until all the others were out of the boat, then joined them on the concrete apron. He looked at them, deploring the scruffiness of their appearance—and his own, he knew, was equally scruffy. But it could not be helped, and it did not matter.

An immaculately uniformed officer was walking towards them. He looked at them with a distaste that he could not quite hide. He stared at the Rim Worlds Navy insignia, the stylized wheel, on the stem of the boat and his eyebrows lifted in amazement.

He asked, "Where are *you* from? And who gave you permission to land?"

"We are castaways, Commander," Grimes told him. "We request assistance."

"And you look as though you need it. And aren't you a long way from your own puddle?"

"That will do, Commander," snapped Grimes, but his authorative manner was wasted. The officer was looking at Sonya, hard.

He said, "I know you. Commander Verrill, isn't it? But we'd heard that you were dead, that you'd vanished on some crazy expedition out on the Rim. But what are you doing here?"

She said, "I'm not quite sure myself. But my husband, Commodore Grimes, is in charge." She stressed the title of rank. "I suggest that you ask him some time, after he has had time to get cleaned up and has made his report to his superiors, and to yours."

The Federation Survey Service Commander was

humbly apologetic. "Sir, I have seen photographs of you, but I never recognized you . . . *The* Commodore Grimes. But you were lost, with your ship, *Faraway Quest*. On the Rim of the Galaxy. Surely you never came all the way here in *that* . . ."

Grimes cut him short. "It's a long story, and I'm not sure that you'll believe us, even if we tell it to you. Meanwhile, please take us to whoever's in charge. My officers and myself are in need of food, fresh clothing, and possibly medical attention. Oh, and you might put a guard on the boat—although I doubt if we will be able to learn anything from the Carlotti transceiver *now*."

"Come this way, sir." The Commander was obviously bursting with curiosity, but restraining it with an effort. "I'm sure that Captain Dell will be happy to make all arrangements for your comfort . . ." Then, "But how *did* you get here?"

Grimes sighed. He would be answering questions and writing reports for far into the foreseeable future. He would have to explain, or explain away, the loss of a unit of the Rim Worlds Navy. He would have to tell the stories of two mutinies—that by Druthen and that by Dalzell. When he got back to the Rim he would have to face a Court of Inquiry.

"How *did* you get here, sir?" persisted the annoying young man.

"We took the long way back," said Grimes at last.